I0847031

REBIRTH
THE TIME GU...
SERIES

G.B. FINN

Copyright and Disclaimer

Legacy Elect Books LLC
113 S. Perry Street Suite 206 #6208
Lawrenceville, GA 30046
Copyright © 2023 by Q. B. Finn
ISBN: 979-8-9877030-8-3

ABOUT THE AUTHOR

Q. B. Finn is a Born Again Christian husband and father who enjoys crossword puzzles, brain teasers, and board games. He also enjoys reading Christian novels and secular Sci-fi, mystery, suspense, and historical fiction novels. He works remotely by day and is an author by evening. He also owns a publishing company. God commissions Q. B. to write books to entertain and minister to readers about Jesus Christ. You can reach him through the various social media outlets below.

instagram.com/legacyelectbooksllc/

twitter.com/legacy_electbks

youtube.com/@legacyelectbooksllc

facebook.com/legacyelectbooksllc/

Contents

Dedication

First, I thank God the Father, Jesus Christ, and the Holy Spirit for the direction and blessing to write this book and other books in the future. Secondly, I also thank my wife for her assistance in editing this book and her encouragement through my ups and downs during the writing process. I also want to thank my son for his input on the cover for this book.

Scriptures and Quotes Referring to Time

"Do not fear, for I am with you; Do not anxiously look about you, for I am your God. I will strengthen you, surely I will help you, Surely I will uphold you with My righteous right hand."

Isaiah 41:10

"I am the Alpha and the Omega, the First and the Last, the Beginning and the End."

Revelation 22:13

"There is an appointed time for everything."

Ecclesiastes 3:1a

"The only reason for time is so that everything doesn't happen at once."

Albert Einstein

"Going back in time has already started a change in the time continuum and simultaneously affected the time portal. How much change? I am not sure. It depends on how many times you venture through the portal."

Professor Albert Hernandez

"Time is unfaithful for those who abuse it."

Unknown

Prologue

April 4, 1865 – 1:45 PM

Dressed as a Union officer, McGee looked at his small, metallic hand-held device's screen and then glanced at each door as he walked down a long, half-lit hallway. He moved closer to a specific office door after his device continuously beeped, hesitated momentarily, then reached for the doorknob and turned it. He slightly pushed the door open.

"Excuse me, sir."

He stopped and looked toward where those words came from. He found a Union officer, who was the same rank as McGee, walking towards him. The officer was yours truly. I stopped because McGee was blocking most of the hallway, so I slid behind him to get through, which was not my original intention. Since there was not enough room to go by, I abruptly brushed against him. He let go of the doorknob, turned around to face me, and then pushed me against another closed door, which didn't open.

"What is your problem, man? You have enough room to walk by. Do you want a fight?"

"Excuse me? I don't want any trouble from you or anyone else."

"Well, you have one now."

McGee stepped up to me with his fists clenched and swung at me several times. I dodged away from McGee's punches.

"Nice try. Is that all you got?"

McGee wiped his face as he gave a wry grin. He took out his 1865 revolver and aimed it at me. He pulled back the hammer, and the cylinder rotated into position. McGee's finger slowly pressed the trigger. I saw the hammer gently moving forward to push the bullet from its cylinder into the barrel. I stood there wondering how to prevent him from firing his gun—frozen for a few moments like a dead duck, with no cover or weapon to stop him. I only had the circular disk in my right hand, hidden from his sight, which could return McGee to our appropriate time.

"Blam! Phish!"

~

"Stop! Stop! This is ridiculous! Are you trying to make us believe you were at the Confederate White House during the year 1865? If your testimony concerns this time period, I cannot accept the storyline and am having difficulty believing it. I heard you were an excellent storyteller, Professor Hernandez, and now I see that's true. I do not believe what you are presenting today is factual. Overall, I don't believe you at all. I have spoken to many scientists who told me no one can travel through time. So, I believe this is a fantasy you made up to justify your actions. Can't you come up with a better story than this?"

The Chairman, Ronald Jones, for the Senate Oversight Committee in Covert Operations, also known as SOCCO, had a mouthful for me and my recordings. I just lowered my head in humility and with a small amount of shame.

"Sir, let me explain."

"No, Professor Hernandez, you have done enough of that today. So, this is your explanation for arresting six citizens from the Arab community and a former FBI agent. This is horse manure. You can do better, sir!"

I look at the Chairman with great concern. I was trying to figure out his justification for such an outburst. Before you wonder what happened after our verbal exchange, let me take you back to the beginning before Chairman Jones' outburst.

My team and I left my NYU lab to stand before this committee to explain how a disrupted and decaying time continuum justified us in incarcerating seven individuals for various crimes. The beginning sometimes has a way of explaining the end of a story than just being the opening for every account. For your sake, this factual, non-fictional story will enlighten the Truth in your heart and give you solace to have a second chance in your life. As the recording will illuminate, the beginning was not pretty because of a submerged memory in my mind and heart until the Light brought it out. I had to learn to deal with that memory. Still, a Voice indicated I don't have to deal with it alone. I narrated a video recording to transition the entire account of our missions dealing with time terrorists and the shifting time continuum. This is a story that contains three stages across various historical periods. I have named them Rebirth, Crossing Over, and Restoration, which I recorded as the only evidence of our actions and orders given to us through the FBI, which ultimately came from the President from 2018 to 2021.

Chapter 1

July 17, 2018 – 9:30 PM

"There are events in everyone's life which may form an enduring, identifiable foundation, which influences and mold you to do good or evil since good and evil exist in the recesses of every person's heart and soul. Whether those events are tragic or joyous, they can shape internal characteristics that will surely last a lifetime. I experienced three events that imprinted my mindset, behavior, and finally, my distinct pain, which rolled over my mind, soul, and heart for the rest of my life."

I had that profound thought as I sat on my sky-blue, wool-blend sofa. You could barely make out the wall panels, let alone the details of the photos on the walls behind and near my plasma TV set. Those pictures showed the existence of joy and innocence during my youth as well as my wife's youthful experiences.

"I wish I could relive those youthful times and never grow up. If only I could remain stuck in that historical period forever. Alas, we all grow old to bear the fruits of our life; hopefully, fully ripen so we can enjoy the sweetness of life and not shrivel up with decay to be tossed away."

I was wearing an Albert Einstein tee shirt, the one in which he sticks his tongue out, with one of his famous quotes. It stated, *"Time is an illusion."*

I've always believed that time was accurate and will always stay objective. Yet the very person who discovered relativity thought that time was an illusion. How is that paradox possible? Does that mean everything we experience is an illusion since we do everything through time? Our very existence depends on time, and God created time. Does that mean Einstein, as well as many nonbelievers, see God as an illusion? These questions were answered through several scientific missions I took with my team.

Anyway, I digressed from the main narrative. That evening, I was also wearing my navy blue Nike shorts while holding my black TV remote in one hand and a small green bowl of potato chips and pretzels in the other. I was glued to my sofa as the light from the TV reflected upon me, and I used that light of mindless shows as a distraction from the pain welling up in my heart. I repeatedly pressed the up and down buttons, flipping through the myriad of channels, looking for anything to fill my emptiness. Yet, I didn't find a thing through the plasma screen as I searched for a needed healing prescription for my ailing heart. After half an hour of flipping through the library of shows and movies recorded on my DVR, I reluctantly shut off my TV set. I was frustrated because I could not fill the deafening silence in my house and shut out the constant loud replaying of the dreadful, frightening events within my mind.

"The first event was the day I looked at my father's magazines, which I found in a wooden box within his work shed. Of course, I flipped through them. They were pornographic, and I was strangely intrigued by those photos. Several years ago, my dad built the shed to create wooden sculptures and different structures, ranging from various shaped planks, columns, large wooden blocks, and dining tables for different homes. He cut and carved those various wood pieces into specific artwork and particular household items, i.e., sculptures, wooden dividers between the kitchen and living room, picture frames, shelves, and bookcases. I expected to see those items and his tools throughout the shed. Instead, I discovered those hypnotic magazines in a toolbox and on one of the bookcase shelves. They contained graphic sexual images which plagued my mind and heart for years. I was an innocent, naïve ten-year-old boy who believed and thought that looking at my dad's magazines would make me more like him and possibly make us closer. Instead, I was appalled by those images forever imprinted into my young brain without any chance for them to be erased; those synapses are still

there. Yet, simultaneously, I was curious about what those people in the photos were doing to each other. No one knew I made that discovery and how it empowered me because others in my age group didn't know. I had one thing over them which they cannot take away from me."

I thought and reminisced about that dreadful scene as I stared at the blank, black plasma screen for a few more minutes; then, I got up and rubbed my forehead, eyes, and cheeks. I was trying to get rid of those thoughts.

"If only I didn't look at those magazines, then maybe my innocence would have stayed secure, void of those deviant thoughts, which haunted me for years,"

I said to myself as I shook off the numbness from my legs, which also ran throughout my whole body, caused by sitting on the sofa during the half-hour TV search. I went to the fridge, hoping to find anything to quench my thirst. I looked past the Pyrex beakers of leftovers and bags of fruits and veggies to find a bottle of wine, but instead, I took the filtered water and filled my glass. I surveyed the kitchen. My eyes passed over a three-day mess of dirty silverware, pots, and pans. Shrugged my shoulders as I shuffled back to the living room and then plopped myself on the sofa again.

"I am such a mess. A few years after that dreadful magazine discovery, a male I trusted adult sexually abused me. He was a family friend who coached the middle school track team, and my parents trusted him dearly. This was the second event hidden deep in my heart and consciousness for many years. The third event moved the sexual abuse to the forefront of my mind and spirit.

As a young man, I sought salvation from those images by attending different churches, i.e., Lutheran, Catholic, Baptist, Episcopal, Methodist, etc. I never found it in them; instead, I found it at the Holy Ghost Church, a nondenominational church in Los Angeles. I went into the church and sat towards the rear of the sanctuary to secretly listen to a message of salvation, which turned out to be excellent. From twelve years old until my early thirties, I searched for a message that could clean my mind, heart, and soul and free me from an unexplainable burden that plagued my heart for most of my life.

I could hear God in my heart and mind during that service. Once the Pastor gave an altar call, I went up to their makeshift altar, repented of my sins, and surrendered my life to Jesus Christ. He is my Savior, my Love, and Who is the Way, the Truth, and the Life, which I believe today. Jesus is the Way of my life."

Tears flowed down my cheeks as I clenched my teeth while that memory flowed through my mind, heart, and spirit.

"That same evening, at home, while I was sleeping, God revealed the hidden sinful event committed to my body and the actual person who committed the crime, which was suppressed within the recesses of my mind for many years. I woke up in a hot sweat. Even though a gentle cool breeze entered my bedroom, which should have cooled me down, the terrible heat from that vision remained after I got up. I cried out to God, 'Is this a dream, or did this abuse really happen to me? And if it did, then why show it to me after all these years?'"

It has been three hundred sixty-five days, and still no answer. I was very angry at God for the deafening silence.

"Come on, Lord! If this is true, why reveal it to me after all those years? In fact, why hide it from me if you plan to reveal it later?"

I yelled as I walked through the living room, trying not to trip over the plastic bins and cardboard boxes throughout the room. I was packed for my grand move to New York City, which would happen in a couple of months. I reached a window to look for a solution or just God Himself. Instead, I found the slow-moving lights of the LA traffic, even during the wee hours of the night. Those lights showed the outline of the LA highways winding through the acreages of land, mountains, and the concrete landscape of LA.

"The hidden event I have revealed to you is the result of a broken man who took advantage of your youth, which was the uncertainty of who you were and your gullibility. It was not your fault, but I am asking you to forgive him. Remember what I did on the cross when I was dying."

I heard God audibly giving me an incredible request, but I ignored it and asked questions about myself.

"What should I do with these thoughts and memories, Lord? Now they are part of me, so how can I exorcise them from my heart and mind?"

I waited for a reply as I braced myself against the windowpane. I stood there waiting for a minute, which became three to nine minutes and then twelve minutes. I slowly shook my head and shrugged my shoulders as I walked out of the living room, and suddenly, He answered audibly.

"Albert, you are to forgive him and give Me your pain, anguish, shame, hatred, hurt, and evil desires. I will heal you from all of it, and you will find security, rest, and joy in Me."

"Lord, this is difficult. I would rather do something about this pain than forgive that evil man."

Once I entered my office, I heard His voice continuing to nudge me, *"Don't do it."*

I stopped in my tracks and surveyed my office. There was no one there to claim that voice. I continued to my ivory-top desk, sat down, and then put on the laptop to perform a search for my abuser. Within minutes, I found Coach Hood not cowering from the past evil actions he performed upon me and others. Instead, I found him coaching boys' and girls' track teams, this time at the high school level. He was still working for Direct Packaging as a delivery person.

"Now, I will do something about my pain and anguish. I pray that what I am about to do will give me peace."

Chapter 2

This cloudless day produced a gentle, soft breeze that caressed my face as I drove my metallic blue Hyundai Sonata to a specific neighborhood in Los Angeles. I found out Coach Hood's route after I called his supervisor and told him I was one of the company's board members observing each employer while on the job. The supervisor gave me Coach Hood's route, I GPS it and then drove to the Copley Place cul-de-sac, where he usually delivers packages between 3:30 PM and 4:00 PM. Once I arrived at the cul-de-sac, I parked in front of 135 Copley Place and waited for the Direct Packaging truck for close to an hour, and he was running late. I removed my gun from the glove compartment, checked the cylinders, and ensured the safety was off. I rubbed the weapon like an owner rubs a dog after it did a good thing.

"He needs to pay for the pain he caused me. I'm sure he did the same thing to other guys for many years."

"Grr!"

A grey truck with orange lettering made out the following: **Direct Packaging – The Most Trusted Mail Carrier in America**, pulled into the community. My heart raced with great apprehension and uncertainty about what I was about to do. I rubbed my face as I tried to remove the remnants of my brief thirty-minute nap, which I took due to sleepless nights. The truck stopped at a driveway with its hazard lights on. After a few minutes, Hood, dressed in his Direct Packaging orange and silver uniform, came out of the truck with two small boxes and left his vehicle running with some crazy rock tune blaring from the driver's side.

"It's him!"

I was still determining how I was going to pull this off.

"Should I shoot him before he delivers his packages or after he finishes his delivery to every home within this community? It wouldn't make a difference, so I decided to blow him away whenever I have a clean shot."

I slid down my driver's seat to ensure he didn't see me. While I waited for his return from his first delivery, I was experiencing unbearable stress as sweat slowly rolled down my forehead until my brow soaked it up. The cranked-up air conditioner did not stop the sweating, so I rolled down the window to get some fresh air, hoping to cool off. My legs shook due to nervousness and adrenaline rushing through my blood vessels.

"I need to end this unrelenting pain right now. Lord God, forgive me for doing this, but I choose to ignore Your Word so I can have relief and peace."

Coach Hood returned to his truck and drove his vehicle through the cul-de-sac circle.

"He is passing two houses without a delivery. Man, is he leaving the community?"

The metallic cranking of the truck's engine grew louder until it stopped at a house across from my vehicle.

"Now I got him!"

I took out my gun and cocked it to fire it quickly. Coach Hood exited his vehicle and walked to a house behind a long line of tall bushes. He had one package under his arm as he manipulated a midsized device. I opened my car door and stood up, leaning against the door with my gun pointed toward him as he walked back to his truck. No one was around to witness what was about to materialize.

"No! Stop Albert!"

I lowered my gun as quickly as I raised it after hearing that audible request.

"Who is yelling at me?"

I looked around and saw no one on either end of the street.

"Whoever it is, do you think stopping me will solve my problem?"

"No! Your issue with Coach Hood will always be there."

I looked around again to find no one in the area.

"Hello, who is out there?"

I put the gun back into my light green camouflage jacket pocket, got into my car, and quickly pulled away from the scene towards the end of the cul-de-sac.

"There is a better way to settle this issue," the Voice said audibly.

I shook my head as I drove away from the Direct Packaging truck.

"What way is better than what I planned to do? He doesn't deserve to live anymore."

"Killing Coach Hood will not heal you at all. Instead, the pain and anguish within your heart will continue to grow because you didn't forgive him."

I continued out of the cul-de-sac and into the main road of an affluent neighborhood called Beverly Hills.

"You may be right, Lord, but killing him now will only ensure he will stop abusing others today and in the future. Yes, it will not heal me at all, but I wish there were a way to stop Coach Hood before he even touched me. Now, how can I do that?"

I drove to Beverly Gardens Park and got out of my car. I walked over to the central fountain and tossed a quarter into it. I watched a group of people riding on their electric unicycles whizzing by me.

"Lord, I need to settle this, or I will have a breakdown."

I whispered as I observed those unicycle riders zipped back and forth through the many concrete paths within the park. After sitting there for nearly an hour, I got up and walked back to my car, wondering how to erase or quench this anguish in my heart.

"I may not have an answer right now, but I will one day."

Chapter 3

July 18, 2020– 3:15 AM

As I tossed and turned throughout the night, I mumbled a few words and groaned while coming in and out of sleep in my New York City apartment. The multiple waves of dreams brought my mind to this new nightmare.

"Hello?" a small voice cried, "I can't see anything! Help!"

That voice moved through the suffocating darkness.

"Is anyone here? Please answer me!" my small voice insisted.

"I am here, Albert!" a more deep, raspy voice replied.

"Oh, thank God I found someone. I am lost, Coach. Can you help me out of this dark room?"

"No problem, just follow my voice, and I will get you out."

I walked closer to the source of that kind, unemotional voice, "Is that you, Coach?"

"Yes, it is, and you're only a few steps from me…Come on over to my side."

"I'm coming, Coach."

I ran towards the source of that voice and reached one of the bathroom stalls.

"How did I get into the boys' locker room?"

I whispered as I approached the stall's door and peered into it. Then suddenly, a hand reached out, grabbed my arm and pulled me into the stall. I then saw a vicious, yellowish grin and red eyes.

"Who are you?"

I could see only an outline of what looked like a face.

"Don't worry; it will come back to you," the shadowy figure said.

Yet, I did not recognize the voice.

A man molested me and then left me in the stall. I blacked out for a few minutes due to the molestation. I shook my head and looked around to find myself on a toilet seat. I thought I was there too long trying to poop. I wiped myself and saw a streak of blood on the toilet paper. I threw the paper into the toilet bowl, which had more paper saturated with blood. I stepped back from the toilet and felt pain in my buttocks. In a flash, a face appeared in my mind: Coach Hood.

I jumped out of our king-size bed and startled Karina.

"What is it, honey?" she said.

"It's nothing. Only another nightmare like the others," I assured her, "But this one revealed the whole hurtful scene."

"Are you ok? What was it?"

"I'll tell you in the morning. Go back to sleep, sweetie."

I kissed her forehead and then her soft, moist lips. I lay there for a few minutes and then turned towards my lovely wife. She was fast asleep, enabling me to get out of bed quietly. I didn't go back to sleep for fear of revisiting that dream. So, I went to my office, stared at my laptop for a while, and shook my head.

"So Lord, I accepted You as my Savior, and yet You have given me this gift of molestation and with it many nightmares. Why?"

I rested my head on the desk.

"You wanted to know why you have been so angry for so many years," God audibly said.

I slowly raised my head.

"Are you telling me that's what happened to me when I was 12?"

"Yes."

"For all my life, I didn't remember that abuse?"

"I protected you from yourself. You would have destroyed your life by going after Coach Hood. Either you would have destroyed your life by abusing al-

cohol and drugs and eventually die, or you would have killed him, destroying your future."

"No way, Lord!"

"You are saved now and can't carry through your desire to kill him, but unsaved, that's a different matter. The proof has been that you could not carry it out for the past two years."

"Then what am I supposed to do now?"

"Forgive him," that small, audible voice encouraged me.

"Back to that? Are you kidding me? I still feel this hatred, but now I know the source of it, and I'd rather deal with that."

"Now, how would you do that, my child?"

"I have an idea."

I looked at many of my sketches strewed all over my desk and picked up one of those sheets as I looked at it intently. I then traced my finger over the outline of a huge image.

"I'll use this machine to restore my life and erase that memory of pain and anguish."

"No! You don't know what you may unleash when you use that machine."

I ignored the voice, investigated my hard drive directory to pull up the specs for my machine, and then typed in a date to start its construction: **July 19, 2020.** I saved it before shutting down the laptop. I then got up from my seat with the sketch of the giant machine. I believed that what I had in my hand would solve my painful problem. I looked up to the blue sky and whispered,

"I will use the Teleporter to remove the abuse."

Each Day

by Falling Away

Each day is new.
  Each present day is distinct and different from the past.
  While the future days are new and different from any other day,
  Each day the sun rises, whether it's cloudy or sunny.
  Each day the sun sets as well.
  Each day the birds sing a beautiful song.
  Each day a baby cries for comfort.
  Each day I breathe in the clean air, which refreshes me.
  Lord, You give us each day, and we do what we want from it
  But we need to give you praise for each day because,
  You give us the sun.
  You give us the moon.
  You give us babies to adore.
  You give us the air to breathe.
  You give us a refreshing new day.

Chapter 4

August 24, 2021– 9:30 AM

I shook that thought, dealing with my firm decision to fix my terrifying past, and opened my eyes to the present in my NYU lab. I then brought my attention back to the schematics of the elaborate machine I invented a year ago, the Teleporter. During the first three months of this project, my team and I built the prototype. It satisfactorily functioned as a mechanism, teleporting objects to and from different parts of the world. Yet, I was unsatisfied with its primary function because I needed more from this machine to solve my ultimate dilemma.

In the next nine months, we built a more sophisticated machine in terms of operation, complexity, and stability to transcend time. A person with an untrained eye would only see a mid-sized complex computer with a console for navigational control connected to a large octagon-shaped bulletproof glassed chamber. Both were tied into a large, curved plasma screen with HD and 3D capabilities. These three pieces, separately or in unison, cannot send any object, let alone any person, through a time portal, while the Time Viewer is the missing piece in solving the time continuum puzzle.

The console was a sizeable black contraption with a Wi-Fi linkage and an encrypted internet linkage to the Time Viewer and other small devices I developed in secret, as well as the glass chamber. Those four pieces working together in rhythm and harmony had opened the time portal.

This linkage made the Time Viewer another way of sending objects or people through the teleporter into past or future periods.

Overall, the console controls the teleporter with every teleport and monitors the energy surges and the signals traveling through the time portal. The heptagon-shaped chamber was composed of bulletproof glass with a steel-plated floor and roof and was large enough to fit seven individuals easily. The chamber also has a locking system that will not allow anyone to suddenly leave their mission if they have a change of heart. The door also has a seal to ensure no interference from the outside environment. The TV monitor was a new addition to the teleporter, allowing anyone in the lab to view the mission and communicate with the time travelers. We could prove Albert Einstein's time travel theories and experience them with a great sense of reality.

The Time Viewer was composed of a large flat screen with complex internal microchips, which can connect with any technological machinery, computer programming, and operating system developed by mankind. So, it can connect with PCs, Macs, iPhones, iPads, and Android devices with great speed and ease. I constructed the Time Viewer a year ago with the sole purpose of viewing historical events. It contained every conceivable historical fact, notable tidbits, and not-so-common facts, with some personal historical information from my friends and me, which I downloaded while developing the viewer's hard drive and functional plasma mechanism.

One day, I was fiddling around with the viewer, you know, when you're curious and want to see how a gadget works. That's how I witnessed different historical events on its screen and discovered several facets of dealing with this small machine. Somehow, I connected the viewer to an energy source, which caused it to unlock a hidden or unverified energized conduit. Later, I called this conduit the time portal for reasons I will later reveal. The second Teleporter had a weak connection with the Time Viewer, and I needed to enhance this connection with the third prototype. I then built a third Teleporter and connected it with the Time Viewer so I could directly interact with the time portal.

A few months ago, I witnessed historical events passing through the viewer's screen with one difference from past observations: I can interact with those events in a very tangible way. I sent objects through a portal and brought them back without noticeable changes in their physical makeup. I transported my dog, Kepler, and he returned with no injury or mutation, so I theorized that humans could also make the same trip without harm or side effects. With that in mind, I constructed a larger bulletproof glass chamber and connected it to the computer complex, the Time Viewer, and the plasma TV screen set.

Even though the connection between the components looked simplistic, they collectively carried out the most complex calculations to send and return objects, animals, or human beings through time. I constructed a mini device, a smaller version of the original, to help me manipulate the Teleporter without being in my laboratory.

I called this mini device the Time Viewer Unit or the TVU; I know, not so original. This new device fits within the palm of my hand. It is black with silver borders and a small screen on the left side, while on the right side, there are three buttons and two levers. Within the screen, a keyboard appears so I can type different periods or regions whenever I want to send myself or any of my team members to a specific time during a mission.

This unit allowed us to connect with the Teleporter and harness its energy to teleport us to and from different periods in milliseconds. The TVU exhibited the same capabilities as the original Time Viewer.

I wrote in my journal.

8/23/2021 – 9:45 AM

"Today, we have conducted two trials with my Teleporter, and little progress has been made. I am waiting for Garcia to inform me that we are ready for the third trial, but I wonder whether we should even try. Unfortunately, several of my colleagues tried to upload the new programs into our office and lab computers, which did not help with the speed of our Teleporter. In addition, I pray that I can succeed with my mission, which can free me from the pain I received years ago. I need to find a suitable time to execute it. If our last trial fails, I cannot carry out what I intended, and I must

wait for another seven months to a year for my entrée into the past. My life and future with Karina may take a hit due to the time and effort I spent away from her due to this dark cloud of abuse I experienced many years ago. I am driven to complete what I set out to do in the hope of restoring my life. If this works, then I may be able to help others in their quest for peace."

A loud knock at my office door startled me, and I almost dropped my journal.

"Yes, come in."

I quickly tossed the journal into my satchel.

"Al, you asked me to get you when we're ready for our third teleport attempt."

Garcia entered the room.

Shelly Garcia joined my team three years ago. More like she stumbled onto my team; I caught her from falling down a flight of stairs in the Main Building at NYU. We talked about the chances of my presence catching her and how I could get to that spot minutes or seconds before she started down those stairs.

"If that's ever possible."

Her eyebrows folded as she looked into my eyes. I smiled as I guided her down the stairs.

"Join my team and find out."

"Are you offering me a job?"

"Yeah, if you want to call it that."

"Ok, I am in."

We shook hands after we exchanged numbers.

Garcia finished her master's in computer programming and certification in CompTIA A+. If I weren't married, I would have been involved with this brunette, petite, spunky, Puerto Rican young lady. Also, my faith and allegiance to Jesus Christ prevent me from having any intimate relationship. From that day onward, we became acquaintances, which grew into a solid friendship through my work with the Time Viewer, Teleporter, and other inventions. When people watched us work together, they thought we were involved or married, but they were mistaken because I had been married to Karina for more than three years. In any case, Garcia had been my most loyal colleague during those years. I absolutely trusted her with the development and schematics of the Teleporter as well as any decisions dealing with the Teleporter, my other inventions, and any missions I accepted for our team.

I got up and walked around the desk.

"Thanks, Garcia. Did you align the energy output from the console to the chamber and Time Viewer?"

"Yes, I did, but the energy levels decreased to 50% when I made the connection. You may be right; we need more energy than we muster to enter the time portal."

Garcia walked over to my office windows and looked towards Washington Square Park. She turned around, crossed her arms, and leaned against that window. I looked at my computer screen, trying to find any energy levels to squeeze out within the numbers provided by our previous tests, and I couldn't find any. I got up and looked at Garcia as I rubbed the back of my head. I was stumped.

"Now, we need to find a way to increase the energy levels within the time portal without destroying it for successful teleportation. Where will we get that energy?"

Garcia walked over to the other window and pulled up its shades.

"Al, you need to let in more light. How can you see anything in this room?"

"Believe me, Garcia; I can see everything."

"What I can see is that we can't mustard enough energy to keep the entire lab running, let alone power a time machine."

"Garcia, you must not refer the Teleporter as such, especially outside our team."

"Yeah, Al, I got it. Sorry."

I got up and walked over to my office's door.

"It's ok. Let's see if we can get some energy from the Time Viewer and route any backwash from the portal."

I opened the door and saw Karina a few feet from the teleporter. Karina and I walked over to each other and hugged, which seemed to last for an eternity; at least, we thought so. Karina and I met at UCLA, and we hit it off immediately. It was as if we had known each other for years. This feisty, semi-dark-skinned, brunette, petite young Dominican lady always delivered her common sense and intellect into our team meetings dealing with the construction and usage of my inventions. She always kept me on my toes.

Three months after I met her, I asked her to marry me. She immediately said yes, and the rest was history. Talking about history, she has a Ph.D. in World and American History and a Master's in Economics, which she taught at UCLA. Her historical specialty has been American History, specifically the American Revolution and all of the 20th Century period. Still, she also has an affinity for European history dealing with the aristocrats, Egyptian historical and social behavior and their art, and Middle East history from before Christ until today. We talked for hours on the day we met on her first day on the staff. Three months after we met, we went on our first date.

We had lunch, watched a movie, and then had an extravagant dinner. That date has continued for us during these past three years. During our time together, we learned to trust each other implicitly and grew further with the Lord. Karina needed help understanding the deep scientific functionality and background of the Teleporter. At the same time, she added the historical aspects of each period we may travel to and the ramifications of our possible tinkering with those events. I am so happy and proud to be married to such a beautiful, trustworthy, and dynamic lady. As we released each other, Karina looked at my expression and continence.

"What's troubling you, dear? You've been a bit distracted lately."

Karina grabbed my arm as we walked towards the teleporter. I did not get a chance to answer as Corey intercepted us.

"Sorry, Al, I didn't mean to interrupt. I just wanted you to know that the teleporter is ready, but I cannot guarantee a successful journey to the past, anywhere or any period, even for three minutes. We need to run more tests before you try this third trial."

Corey Anderson joined my team three years ago, practically a day after Garcia came aboard. His Scottish background gave him the grounded certainty of his work, but he also has a solid loyalty to the people he worked for these past few years. He stood at six one with a lean muscular build; maybe he was a basketball player or a distance runner once. I do not know, but he can handle himself on the basketball court whenever we have a pickup game. Overall, he never presented himself as a physical threat to me or anyone else on the team. He has a Ph.D. in Computerized Physics, Quantum Time Theory, and Engineering. As Garcia was the brains of the tec teleporter's tech programming and syntax development, Corey was the engineer of its physical construction, the internal electronic mechanisms, and the machine's electrical and physical makeup.

After we unveiled the device to the scientific community, Corey tweaked and molded improvements into the machine. He didn't believe the Teleporter was perfect in its appearance and performance. I kept telling him there must be an endpoint to the revamping machine. I know Corey meant well in his suggestions, and I was impressed with his work dealing with our machine and any of my other inventions, but he needed to relax with the constant overdrive in tweaking them.

"Corey, don't worry, my friend; it will work. I feel it in my bones."

I patted him on his shoulder, turned to Karina, and hugged and kissed her.

"I'll see you from the other side, and I may bring back some souvenirs."

"Al, you can't bring anything from the past to our present period."

"Corey, I know that. I was kidding."

I released Karina and walked into the glass chamber, signaling my team with a thumbs up. Wilma closed the chamber door and clicked the external lock.

"We are clear from the door, Garcia!"

Wilma Lee was our recent addition to the team. She was a young, brunette, petite Filipino lady who needed to prove to us that she could do any work or assignment. She asked many questions but was a good fit dealing with the Teleporter. I called her the retro girl because she always wears funky vintage clothes from the 1980s. Overall, Wilma had relieved the workload and pressure from my top techs and the rest of the team by taking on the non-essential and low-priority assignments originally earmarked for my high-ranking techies.

"Got it!"

Garcia pressed a red button on her console to secure the internal lock of the chamber's door. Only a code sequence from Garcia or the chamber occupant can unlock that door.

"Ok, guys, it's a go. Everything checks out. In 10, 9, 8, 7, 6, 5, 4, 3, 2, 1, teleport!"

Garcia pressed the teleport's green button. A zapping sound came from a colorful opening that formed above my head. Red, green, and blue charges entered the chamber, enveloped me, and I disappeared in a blink of an eye. I heard Karina gasp as I entered the time portal. Instantly, I felt a tremendous force tugging at me, shifting my presence from one time period to another. The force grew stronger with every passing second, yet I did not lose my sense of balance or consciousness due to that force. A rumbling sound, like a food processor grinding those edibles to a good, smooth mixture, echoed throughout the tunnel. I was able to look to my right and left without restricting my head movements. I did it several times until images on the moving tunnel wall caught my eye.

"Now, when and where did I experience this visual effect?"

I rubbed my chin, and then I got it. Whenever I drove through the Long Island Expressway at high speed, the soundproofing walls gave the illusion of a tunnel. I am sure you had the same experience while driving through your respective highways in your town or city. My attention returned to the time portal wall, and I tried to record the different images on those walls with my Time Viewer Unit.

"I hope I can save these images, or my team will not believe what I am seeing."

"Karina, press it now!"

Garcia shouted to knock Karina back to reality. The shock of her husband's sudden disappearance and entrance into the time portal was a bit much for her. Within seconds, Karina shook her head and looked at Garcia.

"Oh, yes, I forgot. Sorry!"

She pressed the stopwatch's green button. As she looked at the empty chamber once more, she prayed.

"Lord God, please protect my husband and, most of all, bring him back. I do not know what I would do without him. I asked this in Jesus' name. Amen."

Garcia and Karina walked over to the Time Viewer to see whether they could find out which historical time I entered, but in reality, they were looking for a needle in a river of a time haystack. The computer didn't record any historical time I entered, which greatly concerned Garcia.

"I thought we would see him in some historical time period, even if he is in our present year, two or three days ago, but nothing."

After three hours, sudden light flashes emanated from the chamber, streaking through its glass panels and throughout the lab. The portal opened as the light flashes intensified. I reappeared in the precise spot when I first entered the time portal.

"Al, you're back! Thank God!"

"Yes, Kari, I'm back in one piece."

She then pressed the stopwatch's red button, "3:15.33."

"How do you feel, Albert?"

Garcia's voice echoed through an intercom within the chamber.

"I'm okay, but I have a story to tell you."

I pressed the release button on my TVU and reached for the chamber door handle when the electrified secondary locks were activated and prevented my exit from the foggy, glass chamber.

"Hold on, mister! You can't leave the chamber until I get your new vitals."

"Garcia, are you kidding me?"

I turned towards her and slid against the chamber wall to its floor.

"It will only take a few minutes, honey," Karina reassured me.

"Ok, fine. Get on with it."

I sat there, remembering why I started this quest to travel through time.

"Now, I must find a way to execute my plan with no one noticing."

"Bleep! Click!"

After waiting for five minutes, the chamber door unlocked, and I exited the chamber a bit miffed.

"So, tell us what you experienced in the great beyond," Karina said.

"Yeah Al, we couldn't track you for any part of those three hours in your journey through time."

"Well, Kari and Garcia, I was traveling through a stream of light that seemed to have no end. Then I heard a voice."

Karina, Garcia, Corey, Wilma, and other lab team members stopped in their tracks. I put my traveling satchel in my cubicle and noticed the stillness of the lab. I turned to them as I tried to explain.

"Yes guys, I heard a voice. It told me that this teleporter would help mankind in more ways than I could imagine. It also told me that the machine would restore lives."

The rest of the team continued working while Karina, Garcia, and Corey walked me to my office.

"I don't know, Al. Are you sure you heard a voice, or was it just your subconscious speaking to you?"

"No, Garcia, it was a distinct voice."

"Was it a male or female voice?"

"It seemed to be a male voice. I am not sure, Corey."

"Honey, was it God's Voice?"

Karina rubbed my arm and then my shoulder. I looked at her and was about to answer when a loud noise came from within the lab. We rushed out of my office to find out what caused the commotion. We witnessed sparks jumping from the lock of the lab doors. I looked at Karina, Garcia, Corey, and then Wilma, and each one showed an expression of concern and confusion. I turned to that lab door and then braced myself for what would come through and enter our lives.

Chapter 5

August 24, 2021– 12:55 PM

The lab door suddenly crashed open, and a group of men and women rushed in with AK 9's pointed toward me, Karina, Garcia, Corey, Wilma, and my fellow lab workers. One of the individuals within the group called out.

"No one moves an inch!"

About twelve to fifteen individuals in that group wore fatigues, berets, gloves, and sunglasses. I slowly raised my arms and turned my palms toward the intruding group in surrender. Everyone in the lab did the same thing.

"Was that necessary? You just had to knock. We would have opened the door. So, who's going to repair it?"

"Professor Hernandez, your door is the least of your problems, but my people will handle it."

"Yeah, that would be great, and you are?"

I lowered my hands, and my team followed my lead.

"I am Eugene Robinson, the FBI Bureau Chief Officer for the Northeast Region. You can call me Agent Robinson or just Robinson. May I call you Al?"

Eugene Robinson, a broad-shouldered, African American man built like a linebacker for the Pittsburgh Steelers, was the lead FBI field agent for the region, as mentioned earlier, stationed in New York City for the past three years. Previously, he was the chief FBI agent in DC for seven years and the police commissioner for the DC police department for three years. Before that position, he was a DC detective for five years and a beat cop for seven years. Robinson craved future promotions and the fame that came with them; he found them more satisfying than anything he had experienced. This time, he sought the FBI Director's position headquartered in New York City and overseeing the entire United States East Coast. He considered each case a possible push for that position.

I extended my hand toward him, and we shook hands. I turned towards my team and nodded towards them as a signal that all was well for the moment.

"Good afternoon, Agent Robinson. I am Professor Albert Hernandez. You can only call me Professor Hernandez. Only my close friends and colleagues call me Al. We are not on that familiar level at this moment, so I hope you adhere to this request."

I then nodded toward Karina and Garcia. Karina pointed her phone toward Agent Robinson to film what may develop during our discussion. At the same time, Garcia pressed a yellow button on the computer console, which triggered a yellow recorder icon to appear on the computer's monitor.

"I knew you were the right person for this mission, and I informed my superiors the same thing. Having your team record this encounter and discussion further proves what I told the President, his cabinet, and the Joint Chief of Staff. I would do the same thing to protect my property, invention, and people."

"What do you mean by 'the right person for this mission'?"

"It seems I am not getting my message through; I hope this will be clearer. I have a mission for you and your team, so we need your machine to complete it. Your mission, Professor Hernandez, should you accept it is a race to save the world. I am such a sucker for Mission Impossible."

"We're not agents nor trained as such. What can my husband do for you in this so-called mission?"

"Your husband can help us stop a terrorist or a terrorist group from changing historical events, specifically, American events. Professor Hernandez, your machine can help us save our country; if you don't mind the drama within me, we can save the world."

"Which machine?"

I turned towards the rear of that massive laboratory and pointed to at least seven machines; six were covered with painter's drop cloth along the room walls, while one stood in the middle of the laboratory with lights flashing rhythmically, emphasizing its importance.

"Your Teleporter is the machine we need since it can bring anyone to any part of history, past or future."

"How do you know about that?"

Robinson confidently stood there with arms behind him, seemingly holding something, not ready to reveal it to me or anyone else. He was wearing a gray fatigue bomber jacket and pants. He wore sunglasses, looking more distinguished than the Men in Black.

"We are the FBI Professor Hernandez. We know more about you, your wife, and your team members than most people can find out. We also know the history of your precious machine."

"Hold on, are you saying those terrorists can travel through time?"

"Yes. Now, do you understand why we need your machine? This is the intel we have so far."

Robinson gave me a folder and directed his agents to secure the perimeter and repair the laboratory's door. He then radioed another team of agents to secure the lobby of the Main Building. Karina and I reviewed the report while Garcia and Corey directed their attention to the Teleporter. I lifted my eyes from those pages and got a glimpse of Washington Square Park. I couldn't help to reminisce about the first year we experienced the Square. We were young, naïve, and innocent with great dreams and aspirations to help mankind through our work. I, for one, was so gullible to believe that mankind can appreciate the beauty of time. Instead, mankind, with their innate evil and prideful heart, always wants to control everything and claim to be the creator of the subject or substance being studied. I returned to the dossier Robinson gave us and continued the incredible read. Once my eyes moved over the last word, I looked at Karina to find a shocked-filled face, which, surely, I was also expressing. I laid the report on one of the desks within my cubicle and then turned to Agent Robinson.

"Ok, how can we help?"

"Albert, does your machine work?"

I cringed when I heard my first name come out of his mouth, but the information I absorbed from the dossier made me realize that I had to let go of my pet peeves for the greater good.

"Yes, we just finished our final trial."

Robinson grinned.

"What do you know! Even your name rules can be changed or ignored."

Karina and I led Robinson to the glass chamber. He examined it and looked at the other attachments of the teleporter.

"This is where we enter another historical time."

"How many individuals can travel at one time?"

"The limit is seven people, yet we haven't tested that theory."

"What and when was your first mission?"

"Our maiden voyage will be the one you are commissioning us to do, Agent Robinson."

He looked wide-eyed at me and then rubbed his goatee.

"Yep, you have picked a team that hasn't proven anything. We believe we can accomplish the mission but lack data to support this faith."

"I understand, but no one else has come close to what you have developed."

I nodded and then looked back at my machine with a private thought, even from Karina.

"Yet my secret mission is just as daring and important."

"Really? Interesting?"

"Al doesn't have to work with Agent Robinson. I wonder what was in that report."

Garcia picked up the dossier from my desk and looked through it as we walked toward the large chamber. Robinson and Karina stood there talking about the unit. I then turned towards Garcia.

"How soon can we prepare the teleporter for our first official mission?"

Garcia shook the cobwebs, placed the folder on her desk, then turned towards her computer and clicked on several screens with her mouse to check the status of the teleporter.

"We should be ready in fifteen minutes."

Robinson overheard and responded,

"Good."

"Agent Robinson, do you know what historic period those terrorists will or have entered?"

"Albert, my team was able to decipher the intel from their unit that they had entered somewhere within the mid-1800s, specifically during the American Civil War."

"Why did they select that historic period?"

"Garcia, it was our young nation's most important historic period. It was when our country would remain one country or split into two countries or many territories. Our countries' weaknesses were exposed during that war. Our young nation would have been destroyed or taken over by other nations waiting for it to become weaker and more vulnerable."

"Now that's interesting, Karina. Maybe that's what the terrorists wanted to ensure, to make America more vulnerable and weaker for the easy pickings."

"Then Agent Robinson, we have no other choice. We have to stop them."

"Um, Al, stop him."

"Him? I thought we were to engage a group."

"No. This person was a former agent."

"Really? What's his name?"

"Gary McGee."

"I hope you have a photo or some details on this guy," Garcia interjected.

Robinson gave them a blue folder.

"This has all the intel on the traitor."

I took the folder and poured it over for at least ten minutes. I passed everything I read to Karina, Garcia, Wilma, and Corey. They quickly looked over the intel and photos, except for Wilma. She stared at the photo as if she knew him. Since we were pressed for time, I didn't pursue it. Yet I kept that image of Wilma's conflicted expression in the recesses of my mind; sometime during our mission, I needed to know why McGee's picture disturbed her.

Once we were done with the briefing, we changed our clothes to the appropriate costumes for the Civil War historic period. Yes, we purchased several costumes for our planned missions to different historic periods each member wanted to visit. Collectively, we wanted to visit Israel during the time of Jesus, the restoration of Israel in 1948, America during the time of the American Revolution, the Civil War, the Gettysburg Address, the Spanish-American War, the 1901 Supreme Court case Downes v. Bidwell, the Great Depression, VJ Day, Kennedy's Assassination, Reagan's Assassination attempt, and 9/11 attacks, Europe during the time of the Reformation, Renaissance, the Spanish Flu, and World War II. Instead, we must save our historical timeline in this mission, or our country and our way of life will disappear. Karina, Corey, my top assistant in the lab, Wilma Lee, and I entered the glass chamber. Wilma fidgeted with her costume,

"I can't believe I have to wear this. These clothes are so uncomfortable."

The rest needed to adjust certain clothing parts to make it feel right. Garcia would have joined us, but she is the only qualified person, other than me, to operate the teleporter and take care of any bumps on the road dealing with the teleporter and our travels, so Wilma was her replacement. Karina and I relied on Garcia explicitly with the correct linkup of the Time Viewer Unit with the teleporter. Wilma worked as Corey's assistant in the construction of the teleporter and assisted with connecting the Time Viewer Unit with other components of the teleporter. Corey vouched for Wilma's abilities and diligent work on the teleporter's construction. Yet, during this mission, I had to keep an eye on her; she was the wildcard in our team.

Each member held hands as I nodded toward Garcia. She started the sequence, which lasted for ten seconds. Robinson just stood there observing the sequence of the teleportation process with no clue what would transpire on the other side. We stood within the glass chamber as colorful lights lit up the chamber and the entire laboratory room, and then suddenly, my group was zapped into the mid-1800s.

"I am out to accomplish more than this mission, yet I will make sure not to jeopardize the lives of my team during my solo task."

I assured myself as I looked at my calculations on my TVU while we zoomed through the time portal. I could not help grinning when I discovered a way to accomplish my mission without my team's knowledge. I looked at the flashing lights and images within the time portal along the portal wall and gave a relieving sigh.

"There is only one way I can do it without risking them or the mission. I hope there are no hiccups during our initial mission."

Chapter 6

April 4, 1865 – 1:30 PM

We fell from an opening in the sky, which most scientists call a void or ripple in space. No matter what you called it, gravity still took hold of us and pulled us from the sky, and we landed on an open field. I brushed off long weeds from my hair and clothing as I got up from that semi-soft landing spot. The rest of the group was finding their bearings as I noticed a grey-bricked building a few yards away from where we landed, which had ivy covering the windows and most of the exposed walls, signaling its lifelessness.

Each traveler experienced different nauseating reactions from their travel through the portal. Since this was the first time traveling for my team members, their reactions after entering a new historical period differed for each person. Corey vomited as the other two team members drank a sugary water mixture to ease their nausea while I chewed gum to do the same. I surveyed the area as the others continued to recover.

Standing in the middle of what looked like a grassy field with a spattering of dandelions and oxalis, I observed puffs of smoke multiplying with every crackling sound. Then, I witnessed a large column of blue-uniformed men surrounding other men with grey or no formal uniform. The breeze picked up, which gave us a whiff of the gunpowder odor. I turned to my colleagues, hoping they saw what I was witnessing.

"Kari, please use your TVU to establish our location, find the nearest city, and what historical period we have entered. Wilma, please find out the population size, the location of their greatest population mass, and what type of vegetation exists in this region, and also map out the area's topography. Corey, please find our terrorist. I'll try to reach Garcia and ascertain the time portal's integrity level and our time frame for our return."

"Yes, dear," Kari responded.

Corey then answered for the team.

"Yes, sir. We will get that to you within three minutes or so."

Now, you must wonder how we can acquire any information without cell towers, satellites orbiting the Earth, or any other internet tools for the intel we needed at the time. Well, we were able to connect with the time portal, which acted like a funnel from the future; it gave satellite connection, cell tower connection, and electrical connection as well. This enabled us to use all of our devices easily. There was a disturbance within the portal.

"Thanks, Corey, for your certainty."

I smiled as I grabbed my device. I pressed a green button near the device's small screen to reach the lab. Karina pulled out the same hand-held device from her 1860s handbag while juggling with her parasol. Each member on this mission has the same device in their travel kit. Wilma and Corey nodded toward me as they moved to a different field section to start their investigation.

"Garcia, can you hear me? Come in, Garcia."

I released the green button on my TVU and heard static as I shook my head.

"Oh, come on, Garcia, we need you now, or we're stuck in this historic period forever."

The static continued for forty more seconds, and then suddenly,

"Al, it's good to hear your voice. I have been trying to reach you for the past half hour."

Garcia echoed with minimal static through the TVU speaker.

"Wow! We just got here."

"No matter. Your vitals are just fine."

"We need the intruder's coordinates. Can you trace his signal or energy source?"

"Agent Robinson gave me his energy signature. I was able to trace his journey and even locate his machine."

"Good, but let's focus on his whereabouts in this historic period."

"You got it, Al. Let me get back to you once I clean up his signal. Garcia out."

I turned to my team.

"We will know where to go in a few minutes. Garcia will soon give us the location of our terrorist, so Corey, can you locate any military movements within thirty miles of this spot? Wilma, can you please trace the highest percentage of gunpowder dispersal within a fifty-mile radius of our position?"

"You got it," they almost said simultaneously.

Karina rushed over to me.

"Honey, our location is Richmond, Virginia, and it's April 4th, 1865."

"Ok Kari, investigate the history 'books' and find out what's supposed to happen in this location on that date. Also, find out the significance of this historic period that a terrorist would come here to alter our historical timeline forever."

"Yes Al, I'm on it."

I took my binoculars from my satchel and looked over the terrain, the buildings, and the landmarks. About ten miles from our position, I saw flashes of gunfire and smoke, *"It looks like a small skirmish."*

I found a small regiment marching from those flashes, but not in retreat. Instead, they were escorting a horse-drawn carriage.

"Who would have the command of a small regiment for an escort? I believe Lincoln would have that seniority and power to do so," I whispered.

"Yes Honey, Lincoln is in that carriage, and I'm sure his son Tad is with him."

"You got something, Sweetie?"

I kept my eyes on the carriage.

"Yep. This is the day when Lincoln and his son enter that building."

Karina pointed to one of the brick buildings, which had a sign with the following inscription:

"**Confederate White House**."

"What's so special about that building?"

"It's the building that housed the President of the Confederacy, Jefferson Davis."

"What will Lincoln and his son do inside the building? It just seems unstable, with just three-thirds still standing. Is it significant to our history?"

"I am not sure, Al. I'll dig up more info on it."

Karina walked away as she looked up different sites within her TVU.

"McGee plans to kill Lincoln and General Grant at this site. I am convinced this is where his murderous plan will unfold," I thought.

"Al, are you there?"

I looked around to see where the question came from until I realized the voice came from my satchel. I quickly took out my Time Viewer Unit and pressed a green button near the microphone.

"Yes, Garcia, what's up?"

"Be on the lookout. McGee should be there within minutes or seconds. Your coordinates have intercepted his route."

"Thanks for the update. Hold on, Garcia, my team is reporting their intel. I'll put you on speaker."

Corey spoke first.

"Al, there is only one skirmish about ten to fifteen miles northeast from here. The Union troops are marching a group of Confederate prisoners into this city."

Wilma then said,

"The air quality has indicated that the large main battle ended two days ago. Small traces of gunpowder within a 15-mile circumference from this spot exist."

Karina rushed over to the team.

"Al, we're at the site called the Siege of Richmond. This is where Lincoln and Tad visited the Confederate White House, and Lincoln sat at Jefferson Davis's desk."

I pointed to the slight regiment movement.

"I was wondering whom those troops were escorting into town. Hey Garcia, you got all of that?"

"Yes, I got that, Al. I've just found your terrorist. He is about to enter your historical period within 10 seconds."

"Zap!"

A flash appeared approximately seven feet from us, and a void opened midair. A young man fell through the hole and tumbled onto the same field we were in. He got up and brushed off the grass, dandelions, and dirt from his uniform. Once settled, he took out a handheld device from his satchel. He tapped the device's screen several times and pointed it in different directions, examining the area. It looked like a Time Viewer Unit.

"How did he obtain the technology I developed these past few years?"

McGee was oblivious to us, yet we hid within the tall weeds. The young man picked up his rifle, gun, and other items that fell out of his satchel. He then walked towards the Confederate White House.

I turned towards my team and whispered,

"My dear friends, the odds are now in our favor. He has no clue we are here, so let's stop him before he changes history."

While we followed the time intruder, I looked at the horizon and enjoyed the blue sky for a brief moment. I also observed the various species of birds flying in erratic directions.

"What's gotten into those birds? Something is about to happen in nature, but what could it be?" I whispered to myself.

We gathered together, kneeling within the weeds to formulate our line of attack.

"Ok, everyone, we need to stop McGee and bring him back within seven minutes, the amount of time it will take for us to be permanent fixtures of history. So, on my mark, let's synchronize our watches for those seven minutes."

Each member of the team complied with my request.

"We may need a diversion, so Kari and Wilma be ready. You may need to delay Lincoln from entering this building any way you can."

They nodded.

"Ok, let's do this."

We got up from our position and moved slowly towards the dilapidated building. We had gotten as close as 10 to 12 feet behind McGee in front of its main entrance.

"Once we're done with this mission, I can get back to the real purpose I built this machine," I thought while we approached our designated positions.

Chapter 7

April 4, 1865 – 1:40 PM

After Lincoln's carriage reached the grey building, two soldiers marched towards the carriage door and stood at attention, facing each other. One of the men opened the door while both soldiers saluted as Lincoln slowly rose out of the carriage with solemn grace. Many reported that he floated out of the carriage or angels carried him out. At that moment, I reacquired my sights on McGee. He was walking with some soldiers and officers into the entrance of the building. I also noticed that he was wearing a captain or general's uniform. I wasn't sure of the rank; this was Kari's area of expertise. The men saluted McGee and didn't question his presence at the building.

I looked at the scene with awe that he had so much ease entering the building.

"Ok guys, we need a distraction, so Corey and I can get in without a hitch. Ladies, are you up to it?"

"Yes dear, we're ready and able."

Karina opened her parasol, leaned it on her shoulder, twirled it, turned to Wilma, still fidgeting with her clothes, and nodded in agreement. They walked up to the carriage where Lincoln stood beside it while speaking to several soldiers.

"Ma'am, you can't go any further."

One soldier held his rifle diagonally across his chest while the other one pointed his rifle toward the ladies.

"Oh, kind sir, we just wanted to see President Lincoln. Can we have a quick audience with him?" Karina said with a Southern accent.

She lowered her parasol so I could get a good view of her position. The soldier looked at both women and then towards his superior.

"Stay right here. I'll see what I can do. Ollie, keep an eye on them."

"Thank you, sir. I want to shake his hand," Wilma said.

She covered her eyes with her fan. She didn't want to give away her Asian features. The soldier went to his captain and spoke about the ladies' request. Karina quickly texted me,

"You're in the clear."

The soldier returned to Karina and Wilma.

"Follow me. 'll bring you to the President."

"Thank you, sir. We're so grateful."

I put my TVU into my satchel.

"Karina just gave us the go signal. Corey, we need to do this quickly without hesitation."

"You got it, boss."

We walked with purpose and certainty right through the building's entrance. The other soldiers didn't even notice us as Lincoln finished his remarks. He then greeted many individuals in the crowd, especially the two ladies from the future.

"Man, I wish I could shake Lincoln's hand. I would have also enjoyed speaking to him. Karina and Wilma will remember this day forever," I thought.

Once inside, we used our TVU scanner to search for McGee. We scanned the hallway and a couple of rooms until we heard a commotion approaching us from behind. We quickly ducked into a room. I pulled the door ajar enough to see Lincoln, Tad, and a couple of soldiers walking through the hallway.

"Wow! Karina and Wilma didn't even slow him down."

Lincoln entered a room with his son as the officers entered another room down the hallway. Once the hallway was cleared, we left the room to continue our search for McGee. Within minutes, we found McGee walking down the same hallway, and then he stopped in front of the room Lincoln entered.

"I will walk by him and place this small beacon on him."

I held up a hockey puck-sized apparatus that was flashing blue light.

"Be careful, Al. I don't have anything to stop him if he attacks you."

Corey quickly put away his TVU.

"No worries. Hold on to my newest weapon, which I developed a month ago. This gun has the same power as a rifle. Please don't lose it."

Corey admired the sleek silver metallic look and feel of the weapon and could see his reflection.

"I will take care of it."

Corey clicked off the safety and stood at the hallway entrance.

Dressed as a Union officer, McGee looked at his handheld device's screen and then at each door as he walked down the hallway. He moved closer to a specific office door, hesitated momentarily, reached for the doorknob, and turned it. He slightly pushed the door open.

"Excuse me, sir."

He stopped and looked towards where the voice came from. He found a Union officer, who was the same rank as McGee, walking towards him. The officer was me. I stopped since he blocked most of the hallway, and then I slid behind him. Since there was not enough room to go by, I abruptly brushed against him. He let go of the doorknob, turned around, and pushed me against another closed door, which didn't open.

"What is your problem, man? You have enough room to walk by. Do you want a fight?"

"Excuse me? Yo man, I don't want any trouble."

"Well, you have one now."

McGee stepped up to me and swung at me a couple of times. I dodged away from McGee's punches.

"Nice try. Is that all you got?"

McGee took out his 1865 revolver and aimed it at me. He cocked the cylinder, and then his finger slowly pressed the trigger. I saw the hammer gently pull back and wondered how I would stop him from firing his gun. I stood there like a dead duck with no cover or weapon to stop him. I only had the circular disk in my right hand, hidden from his sight, which can return McGee to our appropriate historical period.

"Blam! Phish!"

~

"Stop! Stop! This is ridiculous! Are you trying to make us believe you were at the Confederate White House during the year 1865? If your whole testimony is along this storyline, I can neither accept nor believe it. I heard you were an excellent storyteller, and it seems that's true. I don't believe you or what you're presenting to us today. No one can travel through time. This is a fantasy that you made up to justify your actions. Can't you come up with a better story than this?"

The Chairman, Ronald Jones, for the Senate Oversight Committee in Covert Operations, also known as SOCCO, had a mouthful for me and my recordings. I just lowered my head in humility and with a small amount of shame.

"Sir, let me explain."

"No, Professor Hernandez, you have done enough. So this is your explanation for arresting six citizens from the Arab community and also an FBI agent. This is horse manure. You can do better, sir!"

I look at the Chairman with great concern. I was trying to figure out why he made such a loud outburst.

"Mr. Chairman, as I stated, these recordings are my evidence for this time shift. This is the only way for you to see what happened during our missions and why we need to take our final mission to restore our timeline."

"See? I see nothing! We have received only audio recordings, which you can fabricate any story with the help of your team."

"Will a visual recording help you ascertain a proper decision for this hearing?"

Mr. Jones froze with a sudden shock and then looked at his cohorts.

"If the rest of this fine committee agree to such a presentation, then I have no reason to object."

Every committee member agreed to have the visual recordings presented in the hearing.

"Ok, Professor Hernandez, you can show us your visual recordings."

"Great! I will need a few minutes to set up the TVU and the recorded materials."

"You have three minutes."

I nodded and waved to Karina, Garcia, and Corey for assistance. We placed the TVU at an angle and turned it into a projector. Corey pulled down a screen that was seven feet away from the committee.

"Ladies and gentlemen, I will continue with the audio recording from where we left off."

The Chairman nodded, and then I pressed a yellow button on the side of the TVU. The presentation continued. One side note: it was bizarre seeing myself in those video recordings.

~

I quickly checked my chest and abdomen for any wounds, and to my relief, there were none. McGee's gun was on the floor due to Corey's accurate shot with the weapon I gave him. Corey smiled at me as I gave him a thumbs-up. The energy force from the weapon momentarily froze McGee's hand, causing him to drop his gun. McGee repeatedly shook his hand as he backed up. He then used his other hand and pressed three buttons on his TVU while sliding her forefinger over the screen of his device. The time portal suddenly appeared. McGee and I grabbed respective doorknobs near us while Core grabbed a staircase railing.

"Leave me alone, or I will bring down the wrath of God upon this place!"

McGee yelled as he secretly pressed one more button, sending an energy pulse into the time portal. Flashes of light shot out from the portal. I tried to grab him, but McGee pushed me against the wall. The portal vibrated and shook violently to a constantly unsettled state, reverberating through that historic period.

"Earthquake! Earthquake!" many soldiers yelled as they ran for cover.

A group of men ran into Jefferson Davis's office and covered President Lincoln and his son. The quake kept me unbalanced within the hallway. The aftershocks didn't help at all until the final one. Then I finally grabbed McGee and slapped the retrieval hockey puck size disc on his back.

"Now, Corey!"

Corey was on the floor due to the quake but was able to press the retrieval button on his TVU. McGee twinkled out of that historic period into that same portal. As he faded from the hallway, he looked at me astonished and shouted.

"You're also a time traveler? You don't understand. We need to stop America! You think this will stop the cause. There will be others after me!"

I took out my TVU, and I spoke into it.

"Garcia, the retrieval button seems to be functioning just fine. McGee has entered the time portal. You should receive him very soon. Make sure Robinson's men grab his TVU before he causes any possible damage to the time portal."

"Yes Al, I got him on my portal radar screen. With his present rate of speed, he should be in the chamber within seventy seconds."

She tracked McGee's travel through the portal upon the plasma screen, which flashed a constant yellow blip. Instantly, he materialized into the teleporter's large chamber to find a host of agents pointing their guns at him.

"We got him, Al. What happened to the portal? My readings indicated that it shifted from its baseline to forty degrees."

"I am not sure what happened, but I'm surprised you also felt it. Let me know whenever it shifts back to its original position."

"Of course, I'll inform you of other portal changes."

"Were the earthquakes evident in your historic period? Were they full power or light tremors?"

"Yeah, we felt light-level quakes over here. They were between tremors and full-fledge quakes. In the meantime, I'll get back to you after we secure McGee and set up the teleporter for your return trip. Garcia out!"

She pressed a button on the console to open the chamber.

"Good. We will wait for your signal."

I rejoined Corey.

"Hey, did you hear anything from Karina and Wilma? Did they return from their little ruse?"

"No, but I will scan the area to find their position."

He took out his TVU and fiddled with the different buttons and levers to get a read on their location. While he was locating the rest of our team, I began checking out my program.

"Now, let's see the status of this program I developed."

I checked it out to verify its functionality and readiness, and then suddenly, Corey approached me.

"I should have received a signal from them, but there is no reply. I don't know where they are right now. I hope they are ok."

"What? We need to find them quickly."

I closed my program.

"Great, this little blip can hamper everything I've planned for the past seven months."

"Hey, Al, are you there?"

"Yes Garcia, what's up?"

"Are you ready to return?"

"I wish I could tell you we're ready to go right now, but Karina and Wilma are missing."

"What? I'll try to get their energy signatures from their Time Viewer Units. Hold on."

"Thanks, Garcia."

I looked at Corey and shrugged my shoulders. Within seconds, Garcia came back on.

"Al, you're not going to like this."

"What is it, Garcia?"

"I found them."

"What's not to like about that? Where's their location?"

"Al, Karina, and Wilma are alive and well."

"Come on, Garcia, where are they?"

"They are at the time of Jesus' Last Supper. I will try to reach them and get their status."

"What? How did they get there?"

"I am not sure, Al."

"Well, that's not important right now. We need to develop an extraction plan. I will start it up. After you get a hold of them, you need to find out what caused them to travel through the time portal without any propagation."

"You got it, Al."

"Corey and I will look into how we will join Karina and Wilma and get back home."

"Good luck with that, Al."

"Thanks. Albert out!"

Chapter 8

Suddenly, a hole opened up in the sky, and two figures fell from it and landed on a haystack with a loud thud. Karina and Wilma got up and rubbed their back and legs, trying to relieve those body parts from the pain they sustained from their fall. They also pulled the hay from their clothing as they looked around for any clues of what historic period they had entered. The moonlight and the canopy of stars were the only sources of light from that pristine evening sky, which reflected the rough contours of buildings surrounding the duo. The rustic buildings indicated that the historic period they entered was not 1865 or 2016.

"Uh!" Karina sighed as she continued to rub her right side and back.

"Ouch!" Wilma hobbled from the haystack.

She tweaked her ankle upon her rapid entry onto the thin haystack. Karina slowly got up and looked toward Wilma.

"Are you alright?"

"Yes. I have a mildly sprained ankle, bruised knee, and back. Other than that, I am ok."

Without much success, she tried to help Karina off the haystack. Once they got a hold of their senses, they witnessed the town's inhabitants rushing through the dusty road and alleyways. It was an isolated frenzy within the town.

"Why are they so much in a hurry? Is there a flood or tsunami heading this way? Where are we, Karina?"

"Let's see what this machine can tell us."

She took out her TVU and released it from its sleep mode. Karina quickly lowered its volume after a few beeps rang out as it returned to life. Within minutes, it showed their location on its screen. She shook her head and then showed the screen to Wilma.

"Jerusalem 33 AD – Passover - The day of the Lord's Last Supper."

"How did this happen, Karina? We were talking to Abraham Lincoln and watched him enter the Confederate White House. Then we're here."

"Yes, I know, we were also suddenly whisked further back in time. I am not sure what caused this trip, but I am sure Al will find us."

"Was there a disturbance to the time portal or time continuum?"

"I am not sure about that either, but I remember an earthquake occurring simultaneously with our sudden journey. Maybe the earthquake was the cause of our unplanned trip here."

"That has to be it, Kari."

"Maybe? Let's try reaching Garcia. She might be able to shed some light on our predicament."

Karina squeezed her TVU tighter and thought,

"I wish Al and Corey were here to answer our concerns with our present situation, but most of all, I hope they are coming to get us and bring us back home."

"Can we contact Garcia or Albert?"

"I am unsure, but it wouldn't hurt to try."

Around them, people were rushing from here to there, trying to reach their destination as if they had a deadline. Wilma slightly shook her head in utter curios ty and bewilderment. Karina brought her device to her mouth during that frenzy to utter a call into the winds of time.

"Karina! Are you there?"

She almost dropped her device.

"Al?"

"Yes, sweetie. I am so glad I can reach you and that you're alive. Are you guys alright?"

"We're ok for the most part but confused. How did the teleporter send us over here without any input from you, me, or Garcia?"

"Do you know where and when you are?"

"We did a diagnostic GPS location, and the device gave us Jerusalem 33 AD – specifically Jesus' Last Supper."

"Garcia was correct with her search; she gave me the same location and historic period."

"Professor, how did this happen?"

"Wilma, we are trying to figure that out. Garcia is looking for any energy surges that might have triggered Karina's TVU. It's the only device between you capable of teleporting you guys through the time portal."

"Honey, the most important question is, how can we get back home? Especially when we are apart from each other."

"Sweetie, we are also working on that very problem. We may have to rendezvous in your time period and then go back home, or we may have to go home from our respective time period. Once I give Garcia your exact position, she will calculate the feasible method. Of course, we must consider our safety and the security of the time continuum."

"Al, are we safe for the time being?"

"Kari, you are safe, but stay hidden until we reach you. We must ensure that you do not cause irreparable damage to our timeline or any historical events. Any changes, no matter how slight or great, may cause us to remain in our respective time period forever."

Karina shook her head as she rubbed her forehead.

"Easier said than done."

"Kari, my device is buzzing. It must be Garcia. We may have our answer sooner than expected. I'll get back to you in a few minutes. Albert out!"

"Ok Al. Please hurry."

A crowd grew as people milled around the square to get home before sundown. Since we found out they were in the historic period of the Lord's Last Supper, Passover would start at sundown. Karina and Wilma moved to an alleyway to avoid any detection.

"It's Passover, and people are trying to get home for their meal. Wilma, we must get off these streets or be arrested for breaking one of God's laws."

"Are you serious?"

"Yes. We need to preserve history. You heard what Al said if we don't?"

Karina led Wilma to an open door to one of the buildings.

Chapter 9

April 4, 1865 – 2:05 PM

"Just great! This sudden and unexpected teleport is another blip to my plans."

Due to this new dilemma, I had to work on my new calculations from 1865 to Jerusalem, 33 AD, and then from 33 AD to my original destination, Oakwood Middle School, circa 1974. I created a separate set of calculations just for our trip to Karina and Wilma and then a separate return trip home, our present time, to ensure a safe one for my friends just in case I didn't get back in time.

"Albert, are we going to travel to their historic period?"

"Yes, Corey. This trip will be very tricky. This is new territory for us, and I hope my calculations are precise and accurate to send us to them and then turn around for another trip to our historic period. I need you to double-check my figures before sending them to Garcia."

"You got it, Al."

I completed seven calculations in ten minutes flat. For a brief moment, I looked up from my TVU and observed President Lincoln exiting the Confederate White House with his son, heading towards their protective detail. Lincoln stopped and turned towards us. He raised his right eyebrow as he looked at us. I quickly shoved my TVU device into my satchel. We saluted him, but he walked towards us. I tapped Corey's arm to get his attention on Lincoln's movement.

"Hello, gentlemen. Have we met before? I truly believe I have seen you somewhere?"

"No, I don't think so, Mr. President. This is our first detail escorting and protecting you, sir."

"Really? You look familiar, and I am good with faces."

"Sorry, Mr. President, we didn't meet until today."

"Ok then, I apologize for the confusion."

"No, sir it's ok."

We saluted again as Lincoln nodded and tipped his hat toward us. He turned to his carriage and got in. Corey and I lowered our arms from that salute and then looked at each other as we laughed with glee due to that sudden historic moment.

"Really strange, Al. How can he say such of thing since this is our first and only meeting?"

"It may mean we will meet him again in another historic period."

"How's that possible?"

"It means instability of the time portal will continue throughout our mission."

"Even with that fact, interacting with a historical character was still a treat."

Corey looked at my second set of calculations and then took out his TVU to confirm them. Afterward, he developed more calculations, which were improvements from my own set.

"Al, I have made a few adjustments to your figures. What do you think?"

I scrolled down to Corey's new calculations and turned towards him.

"Yes, this will work. Good job, Corey. Thank you for catching my errors."

"No problem, Al. This is one of the reasons I'm with you: to catch your errors."

Corey smiled.

"Oh, I need to ask you something."

After reviewing his corrections, I looked up from my TVU screen.

"Sure, Corey. What is it?"

"Why is there another set of calculations that may lead us to a different historical period?"

"Oh, I was fiddling with other possibilities or scenarios related to this mission."

I bit my lip with that lie.

"I can't believe I sent him the wrong set of calculations."

"Well, be careful, Al. If you accidentally trigger these numbers, we may enter a different time portal without warning."

"Got it. Yeah, you're right. Thanks for the warning. I won't touch it."

Albert swiped his screen to those other calculations.

"Until I need to."

We walked to the same clearing where we first entered this historic period. I tested the different calculations for our rescue mission. Then, I developed three more to make sure we had all the possibilities to retrieve our other team members and return home safely without changing the timeline. Once I completed the three new calculations, I sent them to Corey so he could test them before handing them to Garcia.

"Gentlemen, what are you doing here?"

A Union soldier came upon us. I quickly hid my TVU while Corey also knelt to cover his device. I turned towards the soldier.

"We are checking the building for structural damage due to the earthquake. I need to record my results for future reports to my superiors."

The soldier looked at the building.

"Yeah, that makes sense, General, but we must double-time it to our unit. We are assigned to escort the President back to Washington."

"That's great! We will join the unit after we inspect the other side of this building."

I swung my satchel over my shoulder.

"Sir, where are your troops?"

"I don't have any men with me, corporal."

"I understand, sir. Well, we will leave in five minutes."

The soldier saluted us, and we reciprocated.

"Yes, we will be there. Thank you."

I looked at Corey.

"We must get to the other side of this building and avoid that soldier and anyone else from that unit. Hopefully, this move can buy us some time so that Garcia can give us the green light for our rescue mission."

"Ok, Al, what happens if they send a search party for us?"

"Hopefully, we'll be in the portal heading to Karina and Wilma by then."

"Yeah, hopefully."

We ran to the other side of the building and sat behind blooming bushes that lined the building. Corey looked out for anyone approaching our hiding spot as we sat there. I sat there staring at my Time Viewer Unit's screen, hoping for a message from Garcia. I rubbed my device a couple of times, like rubbing a lantern in the hopes of stirring a genie out of it. Truthfully, I was hoping the device would spit out an equation to help us reach Karina and Wilma. As I sat there, I thought,

"Man, I remember when I came up with the design for this unit. It was just like

yesterday."

~

I came into my lab in a huff.

"Garcia, I need you to see these calculations and this design for my new machine."

She was soldering two microchips within the motherboard of a new computer I developed a few months ago. She barely moved when my booming voice suddenly came into the lab.

"Al, you're lucky I don't startle easily, or we would have to trash this motherboard and any hopes of building the Teleporter."

"Oh, sorry, Garcia. I'm just pumped up with my new invention. I just built this machine a couple of days ago, and I wanted you to be the first person to look at it and test it out."

"Ok, ok, let's take a look at it."

Garcia took the papers and spiral notebook I was carrying. She paged through them for what seemed to be an eternity.

"I wonder whether my notes make any sense to her."

Garcia went through the short stack again.

"Unless she can't make any sense of my handwriting."

I rubbed my forehead.

"Well? What do you think?"

I pleaded with her for any positive sign. Nothing, except for her index finger pointed upward to signal for silence. I then gave her my prototype machine. It was smaller in scale than my original sketches but one hundred percent operational. She examined and played around with the prototype for approximately twenty to thirty minutes.

"Al, this unit looks interesting."

"What's so interesting about it?"

"It looks like a tiny, high-level computer. I have not seen anything like this in my life."

Garcia turned the device over and over a few times to find nothing out of the ordinary. Nothing came of her examination except more questions.

"Hey Al, what's the purpose of this unit?"

"I call it the Time Viewer Unit, or TVU for short."

"TVU? Huh uh?"

"Ok, I know it's a corny name, but the name describes its function. This machine allows you to view different historic periods in history."

"That's nice, Al, but how is it going to help the Teleporter or even help our ability to time travel?"

"Well, I can download specific historical events into this unit and store the data on its hard drive for future trips."

"Really? Which events did you pick?"

"I inserted events I have been interested in, which intrigued me for some time. I also put in events in which Karina is an expert."

"Ok, and they are?"

Garcia raised her hands as she shrugged her shoulders.

"Right. These are the following."

I gave her a small sheet with a scribbled list. Garcia took the sheet from me and read the following,

"JFK and Lincoln's assassinations, Reagan's assassination attempt, American Revolutionary and Civil Wars, Space Age race, 9/11, Industrial

Revolution, the Renaissance, the Roman Empire period, World War I and II, the Bible, Israel's rebirth, and other scientific discoveries."

"Al, what do you mean by the Bible?"

"I downloaded all historical events that were recorded in the Bible."

"Really? Why? I thought most of those events were fictional."

"No. Many archeological finds have validated many events mentioned in the Bible."

"Ok fine. What's so great about viewing all of those events you listed?"

"Garcia, we can select a specific historical event on this TVU, pour energy into that date, and link it with the portal energy from the Teleporter. This will open a door into that historic period and send a person or a group of individuals to a specific day and hour within the selected event."

"What? Are you serious?"

"Yes, I am."

"How does it work?"

"We would pick a historic period, say the American Civil War, through the TVU. We would select a specific date and time for that historic period. We then feed our selection to the Teleporter, which will accept it and imprint it into the unit's motherboard. Then, as we initiate the Teleporter, an energy surge will enter the chamber and open the time door or portal. Within seconds, the chamber's occupants will be zapped into the portal traveling to the selected historic period."

Garcia sat back in her chair and rubbed her forehead as if she had a migraine headache for hours.

"That's great, Al. You just developed a machine that makes the Teleporter functional as a time machine. Wow! I didn't think it would be possible."

"Garcia, we need to test the linkage ASAP."

"I agree. Let's do it later this afternoon. Will that work for you?"

"Yes. Let's say around 3 pm, ok?"

"Yeah, that would be great."

I stuffed my TVU and the sheets with my calculations from Garcia into my satchel.

"I'll tell you how we can specifically set up the hookup between the TVU and the Teleporter."

"Sounds great, Al."

"I'll see you in a couple of hours."

~

I snapped out of that memory and touched the TVU's screen to open a window for telecommunication and another window to read the energy level of the portal.

"Garcia, we are ready to make our historical trip to our present time period and rendezvous with our other team members. Are you ready at your end?"

"Yes Al, conditions are optimal for teleportation."

"This is historical, along with my unscheduled pitstop."

I inputted my other set of calculations into my TVU as a stopover, like using GPS to map out a restaurant as a stopover during my desired journey.

"Now we will find out whether time is fluid and flexible."

Chapter 10

Robinson took out his teal iPhone to review his last communique with one of his agents as he walked past the mechanical techs from his bureau who were repairing my metallic lab door. He raised his head from his phone to find Garcia at the Teleporter's console, looking at multiple screens containing letters and numbers.

"Now, what is she up to? The team should have been on their way to this time period or materializing into the Teleporter's chamber right about now."

He shook his head in disbelief.

"I hope she has some good news for me."

Overall, Robinson was relieved to be out of the FBI building, especially after attending a briefing about this supposedly simple mission they gave me to succeed or fail.

"Garcia, what is the group's status?"

"The team," Garcia emphasized, "has split up."

She put down her scenario journal on the Teleporter's console. Robinson stood beside her, looking at the computer screen and the large TV monitor, trying to understand what he was observing.

"What? Why did they split up? Was there another mission I didn't know about?"

"No new mission, sir. It was not their decision. An energy surge from the time portal suddenly pulled Karina and Wilma further into the past."

"How far into the past?"

"The time period is 33 AD. They are in Jerusalem during Jesus' Last Supper."

Robinson lowered his iPhone and stared at the large screen, which showed no activity. He cleared his throat and looked at Garcia.

"Wow! Can we get them back without disturbing our timeline or any historical event?"

She looked away from him and tried to gather her emotions and thoughts.

"We are trying to do just that, sir."

He took a few steps towards Garcia, stopped, and looked at the computer screen. He didn't know what to do except ask the obvious question.

"What is the status of Albert and Corey?"

"They are fine for now. I've been trying to bring them back with Karina and Wilma to our time period or each pair separately. Albert and I are developing formulas on how we can accomplish either scenario. Ideally, I would want them to return together."

Robinson put away his smartphone before he finished reading the new communique.

"Why?"

"It will take more energy from our system to have separate return trips, and right now, the time portal is unpredictable. The energy levels of the portal have been all over the place, and the structural makeup of the portal has been unstable ever since Al teleported McGee to us."

Garcia continued to punch her calculations into her computer, TVU, and another device Robinson didn't recognize to run a trial scenario.

"Interesting? Is there a correlation between McGee's return and the instability of the time portal? I am just spit-balling here."

"Agent Robinson, we are trying to figure out how to get them back together as one team and then investigate what caused this disturbance, in that order. I need to contact Albert so that we can confer on our calculations. I believe together we may be able to solve this problem."

Robinson tapped Garcia's hand, which was moving the mouse. She took her eyes off the computer screen and looked intently at him as he turned to her.

"Hold off from calling him. Give me at least three specific scenarios to bring your friends back to our present time."

"Sir, why would we do that? I am close to ...."

"Garcia, do it right now. We must preserve our time period at all costs, either by losing our place in history or losing some people in history. Are you with me?"

Garcia looked down, and then her eyes met Robinson's.

"I will try to develop three scenarios for the safe return of the entire team."

"Remember, the priority of this mission is to preserve our history and this timeline."

Robinson took out a stopwatch. Garcia folded her eyebrows.

"What's with the stopwatch? Is he going to time me while I prepare my scenarios?"

"If we can't get them back in any manner within the next hour or two, then we need to close the time portal."

"What? Mr. Robinson, if we close the time portal, we ensure a timeline shift."

Garcia saved her newly developed calculations into her computer, TVU, and a strange new device I developed before this mission.

"I need to hide these calculations before Robinson or one of his techies acquire them and try to stop me from saving my team."

"Are you sure? How can you tell whether there is a change in our timeline?"

"You would witness a shift with people you know. Those people would either vanish or not even know who you are. Unfortunately, simultaneously, you would think everything is normal as you live through the new timeline."

~

"Professor Hernandez, is this the evidence we should seek to prove your claim that we're in the wrong timeline?"

I stopped the playback and stood up as if I was about to teach one of my classes a lesson.

"Mr. Chairman, Garcia's explanation at that time was only for a momentary shift due to a slight disturbance with our timeline. What we have experienced, due to McGee's actions, is a close dismantling of our entire timeline. I am presenting my case to get the green light to reverse this egregious act against our history, in fact, against the world's history."

"Fine, Mr. Hernandez, you got our attention. Please continue with your presentation, and it better be convincing."

I continued the playback as I looked back at my team. Karina smiled and nodded, but I knew she was going through the motions. Even my wife was unsure of my claim, and I don't blame her. I mean, how can you see a change in the time continuum when you have been witnessing everything you are accustomed to as status quo?"

~

Garcia pressed three green buttons on her device, and then a voice crackled through.

"Hey Garcia, can you read me? What's the verdict?"

"Al, you're so right about our chances. We should do scenario three and cross our fingers."

"Hey Albert, are you and Corey alright?" Robinson interjected.

I ignored him.

"Got it, Garcia. I fully agree. Let's do the third scenario, but remember to use frequency 7."

"I will. Thanks, I almost forgot."

Garcia muted her conversation with me to deal with Robinson and his questions.

"What's frequency 7?"

My nonreaction to his question miffed Robinson. He then looked at the text he had just received.

"Prisoner McGee is not saying anything about the mission, but he mentioned there's a team ready to go to the past if he fails."

"Ok. Good work. Give him refreshments and make him comfortable. I will be there in a few minutes to interrogate him. Keep me posted of any changes,"

Robinson texted back.

"Frequency 7 is the energy level we need to reach so we can teleport both groups from their respective time periods with a simultaneous entry into the time portal."

Garcia had to lie to secure the integrity of the rescue mission.

"Really?"

Robinson sensed that Garcia and I were up to something.

"Right now, we have two options in what has become a rescue mission."

"What are your options, Garcia?"

She started to explain the options while also texting me them as well.

"Option A is to have Albert and Corey travel through the time portal. As they reach the Last Supper time period, Karina and Wilma will join them to enter another time portal after receiving a signal from Albert to join them. Timing is crucial in this scenario. Then all of them will return home."

"That sounds tricky. What happens if Karina and Wilma miss Albert and Corey?"

"Albert and Corey will continue home while Karina and Wilma enter another time period in ancient Israel."

"Wouldn't history change if those two ladies remained in ancient Israel?"

"I am not sure, but we shouldn't settle with that option because it's the easiest way out of this dilemma."

"Then what's the other option?"

"Option B is a better scenario but also tricky in terms of both groups locating each other. Eugene, Albert, and Corey will enter the Last Supper time period and rendezvous with Karina and Wilma. They then return home together with a new calculated sequence. In this scenario, they have thirty-three minutes to enter the time portal for their return trip."

"What happens if they try to enter after thirty-three minutes?"

"The portal will close after that time, and they will be stuck in ancient Jerusalem or somewhere in Israel for three days. After that, we can send a rescue team to get them back."

"Well, tell Albert he has the best chance to get back home with Option B, but don't tell them we won't send a rescue team if they fail."

"What? We can bring them back, sir. We need a few days," Garcia insisted.

"It is better to sacrifice four-time travelers than to send more individuals through a time portal compromised by something you haven't or can't identify. You even admitted to its instability and unpredictability whenever a person is teleported through it. Our priority in this matter is to preserve our history, so we will do it this way. We then must destroy the teleporter to ensure no one will try to get them or for anyone to have a chance to tamper with history. Lastly, we must destroy McGee's teleporter and other similar models we may uncover."

"If you think that's the best, sir. I want to go on record that I can't entirely agree with your decision, and we must rescue those four time travelers, my friends. As for the other machines, we can neutralize them from here once we have their locations and activation code numbers."

Garcia turned the transmitter dial to seven, allowing us to communicate only with each other while cutting out Robinson. This will also deny his agents the ability to detect the transmission, let alone hear it.

"Duly noted, Garcia."

Robinson walked to another computer a couple of feet away from Garcia. He fiddled with it for a few minutes.

"I am sure he is trying to get access to our teleport info or our immediate conversation."

Garcia turned to her TVU and typed her message to me.

"Al, Agent Robinson has ordered me to inform you that we should do Option B."

"Ok Garcia, I agree with him for the first time."

"One small caveat: you know you have a thirty-three-minute window to return home and a three-day window for us to rescue you and the rest of the team if the first attempt fails. Robinson said he

would close the portal by destroying the Teleporter if you guys don't make it the first time around. This will leave you stranded in ancient Israel forever."

I froze for a few moments.

"Then I need to do whatever it takes to get us home. Garcia, you need to help me in any way; we may have to cut corners to accomplish this task."

"I understand, Al, and I am with you through and through."

"Tell Karina about our new communique frequency and patch her in."

"You got it."

Within seconds, Karina and I were communicating without Big Brother eavesdropping. Robinson left the lab to continue his conversation with his soldiers and superiors, then left the floor as quickly as Garcia patched into our conversation.

"Hey guys, I came across a solution to our problem. What do you have, Al?"

"Of course, I have something as well, Garcia. I bet it's the same solution I discovered through my last scan of the portal."

"You guys always compete for first prize, but this is not the time," Karina said.

"Sorry, dear. Ok, Garcia, what's your solution?"

"Al, we can teleport you and Corey to Karina and Wilma as they start their teleport sequence."

"Once we get there, we will enter into their time period and immediately jump into their energy surge, moving through the new time portal entrance Karina will open, which should take us home."

"Right, Al. We must do this quickly before Agent Robinson gets wind of our plan."

"You're right. Start the process at your end, and I will do my part here. Kari, set up your timing sequence."

"You got it, babe."

Karina quickly took out her TVU and got to work.

"Guys, let's get back online in three minutes."

"You got it, Al."

"Will do, Honey."

I looked at my Apple watch, set the timer, and signed off.

Chapter 11

April 4, 1865 – 2:15 PM

"Now I need to hide my other calculations from Corey. He is smart and can figure out what I plan to do after our mission. I am sure my response to his query about those calculations didn't perturb his curiosity."

I swiped through the Time Viewer Unit screen to examine the total teleportation formulas I developed throughout this mission and my other calculations. I encrypted a sequence folder to save those formulas and calculations, with a password to ensure Corey didn't tinker with them. I turned towards my lab assistant and noticed him talking into his device.

"Garcia, do we still have a duplicating program running for every formula, calculation, notation, and individual changes made to the teleporter, and do you have access to it?"

Corey spoke to her on frequency 3.

"Yes, we do, Corey."

"Can you trace any new formulas developed by Albert or any scenarios he may have written for a destination into another time period other than the one we will travel to? Please look through those records for the past three to seven months. I believe he has been up to something for several months, like a personal agenda."

"No way Corey! Al is as religious in not tinkering with time events as he is with his own belief in God. In fact, his personal life has been spotless. I can't imagine anything he needs to take care of dealing with his past."

"Please satisfy my curiosity and get back to me on this frequency."

"What's with all the secrecy? Why don't we ask him?"

"I don't know if you noticed, but Al hasn't been himself for the past few months. Some pressure has built up through that time period, and it seems he is about to explode. I am surprised you don't see it."

"Come on Corey. He has been under pressure to get the teleporter up and running. I have noticed that for these few months, but I'll check this out to settle your concerns. I still believe it's nothing. Garcia out!"

Garcia did what Corey requested with one thing she whispered to herself,

"My feelings for him must have clouded my sixth sense about people and their behavior. I do love him, but I need to step back and see what Corey is warning me about our fearless leader."

I tried to find the frequency Corey and Garcia were using. Instead, I found three different frequencies emanating from Garcia's device.

"I gotta give it to her; she knows how to cover her tracks."

I walked over to Corey as I switched to the rendezvous calculations I had developed for the past few minutes.

"What's the latest with Garcia?"

"Hum? I was checking the energy levels. She said the levels are still stable, and we should take this opportunity to reach Karina and Wilma. The window of teleporting back

home is decreasing with every elapsed second."

"I thought so. Please review some calculations and run them through your device. I want to make sure I didn't make a mistake."

Corey reached for my device, but I quickly pulled it away from him as if some deadly virus infected him. Is everything alright with you?"

"Yeah, I am just slightly edgy due to our present circumstances. I will send my calculations to you."

I pressed several buttons, and my calculations zipped to Corey's device in seconds. We then leaned over the edge of the building to observe the position of the troops in front of the Confederate White House. They were moving out, escorting Lincoln's buggy. In the distance, other troops were marching toward the smoky remnant of cannon fire. Corey and I could hear the distant booming, which meant the Confederates were not giving up.

"What a simpler and treacherous time. The romance of living in this time period has many drawbacks. Yet, I long for a simple life without the internet, social media,

smartphones, tablets, computers, and other technological inventions. Funny how the teleporter has enabled us to travel to those simpler days. How ironic!"

I chuckled as I pressed different icons on my device's screen.

"Buzz!"

Corey's TVU vibrated. He swiped the device's screen to open the text message app.

"Corey, are you sure AI plans to travel to a different time period? I have checked his system and can't find any program, calculations, or notes to that effect."

Corey quickly typed his response.

"Yes, I am sure, and I believe he will use this rescue event to teleport into another time period. After the three of us start traveling back home, he will make his move, which is the best moment to take the sudden excursion. Looking through his rendezvous and new calculations, I realize I cannot stop him."

"Corey, I can't stop him at my end either. If he does this risky venture, he needs to know how much time he can use in the other time period to ensure his safe return home and the stability of the time continuum. I will tell him the risks of attempting this solo trip somehow."

"Hopefully, he receives your warning with some understanding and wisdom. I pray that his trip will not jeopardize our historical timeline."

"Pray? How can prayer help anyone?" Garcia typed.

Corey shook his head and responded.

"Never mind, Garcia, I am just relying on God for assistance and guidance regarding AI's possible misguided travel."

I observed Corey's frantic, quick typing.

"I wonder what's Corey telling Garcia. I hope it's not about my mission."
Corey approached Albert.

"Both calculations will work, but which one will you use?"

"We will use the long string algorithm to meet and gather Karina and Wilma and then use the shorter one to enter the portal once more for our return home quickly. I already discussed it with Karina and Garcia, but Agent Robinson has been left out of the loop."

"Do we have enough energy and time to execute this rescue mission?"

"No Corey, we don't. We need to pray for a miracle because we will need one."

Prayer

by WWJD

I pray during the morning
 I pray during the night
 I pray in desperation
 I pray with all of my might
 I pray every time I need You
 After my prayer, my heart is solemn
 I tried to find joy, but it was not there
 Is it the lack of prayer?
 Or is it a lack of faith?
 I go to my closet and beseech You for answers
 I know You hear me
 But I don't stay quiet to hear Your Voice
 Which is in the silence of that space
 After my prayer, my heart is moved
 The joy is coming, but not quite there
 Is it my prayer?
 Or is it my faith?
 Now I talk to You unceasingly
 But I don't hear Your Voice when I stay quiet
 We are friends like You and the Prophets

We walk and talk together
You comfort me.
After my prayer, my heart is rejoicing
Joy in my heart is present every day
Is it my prayer?
Or is it my faith?

Chapter 12

"Al, are you there?"

Karina spoke through her small device as she and Wilma hid along the side of a grayish, brown building near the haystack where they had landed a few minutes ago. Sunset had completed, and the sky welcomed the stars in full view. Fewer people were rushing home as the time approached Passover. Karina and Wilma saw several men entering another building with baskets containing linen for a table, plates, cups, and large amounts of food. The duo avoided anyone who may notice them since their outfits didn't fit that time period. One man didn't carry a thing as he entered the same building.

"He must be Jesus," Karina thought.

"Why isn't Albert answering, Karina?"

"He will answer soon. Al, Corey, and Garcia are just working out the calculations and getting the kinks out. They want to get it just right so we don't have any hiccups in recovering us."

Karina's device buzzed.

"I will connect with you in a few minutes," I texted.

She typed on the TVU screen and pressed the send button.

"Ok. Thanks, honey."

"I told you, Wilma. He wants to make sure they will get it right."

Karina showed her the text message.

"Good. I can't wait to get home."

"Don't worry. We will be home soon."

Wilma nodded.

"Hey Kari, what's going on in that building? Many people have entered, and no one has left for the past few minutes."

"I believe Jesus and His disciples are setting up for their Passover meal, which will be Jesus' last supper with his close followers."

"Really? Is it alright for us to get closer?"

Wilma moved toward the end of the alley.

"No! We have to stay right here and wait for Albert's signal."

Suddenly, Karina's TVU rang and vibrated simultaneously. She quickly silenced it while answering the unit.

"Yes honey, what's the verdict?"

"The verdict is closer than I would like it. The amount of time and time distance will be very close for our entry to your time site and then a quick turnaround into another time portal for our trip home."

"Al, is there any other way to get us home without an accidental chance of disturbing the historical timeline?"

"Wilma, this is the only plan that will work with minimal to zero disturbance within the time continuum."

"Al, what are you saying? Will our trips through the time portal destabilize the time continuum further?"

"Kari, I am not sure. The first trip will cause a shift in the time continuum, and the second trip may cause a bigger shift, or neither trip will cause any shift within the continuum. It's like rolling dice. We don't know what we will get until we see the results of the roll."

I signaled Garcia to join their conversation.

"Let's do it and trust God that our plan will work without a hitch."

"I agree, sweetie. Hey Garcia, are you there?"

"Yes, Al. I am here, and we can talk freely. Robinson is not present but will return at any moment."

Garcia's voice boomed through my TVU's speaker. I quickly lowered the volume as I returned to the bushes lined up along the wall of the Confederate White House. Other infantrymen were marching right in front of the makeshift White House. Corey checked whether any of those men within the infantry reacted to the sounds from my TVU. To our surprise and relief, no one heard a thing.

"Understood. Ok team, here's the plan. I will send an energy pulse to Karina's TVU. This will signal our actual entry into the time portal. Kari, once you get the energy pulse, inform Garcia that you received it. Garcia, it would be best if you revved up the Teleporter in anticipation of our arrival after Kari contacts you. Wilma, please start the countdown sequence for seventy seconds as you send the accumulated energy pulse for your time portal entry. At that moment, Corey and I will enter your time period to join you guys for our trip back home. Any questions?"

I sounded anxious and precise, hoping I didn't confuse my team.

"Al, I got it. I will be ready," Garcia replied.

"Honey, will you arrive on time to enter our time portal for our return trip home? It just seems that the transfer from one portal to another within a distant time period is tight. So tight that there can be no wiggle room for any slight error."

"Kari, don't worry. We will have enough time unless there is an unexpected surge of energy drainage within the portal during our teleport. In that case, we will have thirty-three minutes to enter the portal on our return trip home."

"Then good luck to all of you. Agent Robinson will be present for an update when you contact me again."

Garcia prepped her computer console and TVU for the imminent trip.

"Thanks for the heads-up, Garcia. You'll hear from me again when I'm with Karina and Wilma. Oh, Garcia, luck will have nothing to do with our success. I will owe it to God."

I turned towards Corey.

"Ok, let's do this."

Corey nodded and started the countdown. I pressed the green button.

"Ok, ladies, it's a go. We're about to enter the time portal."

"Copy that," Karina and Garcia said at the same time.

Suddenly, a zapping sound crashed through due to the opening and closing of the time portal. Corey and I were pulled into it with one giant swoop.

Chapter 13

"Their trip will take some time since they have minimal energy between their Time Viewer Units and the time portal tunnel."

Garcia bit her lower lip, her usual stressor tell sign. She couldn't help it since her friends were traveling through a compromised time portal, and it didn't matter whether their destination was circa 33 AD or any other time period. She wasn't sure whether we could accomplish our untested time travel rendezvous. Garcia stared at the computer screen, barely breathing and observing the energy readings on the corner of the screen for their first travel through the rendezvous time portal. For a quick moment, she took a glance at her stopwatch.

"Over one hour and counting."

Garcia rubbed her old-fashioned stopwatch, which her father gave her after winning the Cross Country State Championship for her college team. She looked at her computer screen after recording the thirty-third time split. She shook her head in frustration and then looked at her TVU for any energy reading. There was not a single blip to be found.

"Where are they? I can't even get a reading on any movement throughout the portal. Are they stuck, or have they entered another time period?"

"Albert! Corey! Are you there?"

Garcia shouted through the teleporter radio mic located on the teleporter's console. She looked at the multiple screens to find no activity on them, while the teleporter's speakers didn't vibrate a sound during those precious minutes. Garcia shook her head and whispered,

"This can't be happening?"

"Garcia! Why is our team late from their return trip!"

Robinson abruptly entered the laboratory by slamming the repaired lab doors wide open, knocking down a framed picture of the lab team and another of Karina and me standing in front of the church we had attended for several years.

"Whoa! You scared me, Eugene!"

Garcia almost dropped her stopwatch.

"One hour and sixteen minutes have elapsed."

"Sorry about that, but I need to know what's happening with our team."

Robinson walked right up to Garcia and stood shoulder to shoulder with her as they looked at the plasma and computer screens to find no transmission from the portal or me.

"This team is Albert's. You don't have any claim on his team. Albert and Corey went into the time portal to rendezvous with Karina and Wilma while Karina started the sequence on her device. They can join Karina and Wilma if the guys get to them on time, which right now seems unlikely."

"What? Is the teleporter working, or is there a malfunction somewhere within the system that we didn't pick up?"

"No malfunction. The machine is fine."

Garcia continued punching in numbers into the Teleporter computer.

"I was able to teleport Albert and Corey through the time portal, but at this moment, it seems I cannot find them."

"What? Unbelievable! I told you, Garcia, only one group can be rescued."

Robinson leans forward to look at the radar and computer screen. He had no clue what he was looking at, but he tried to fake it.

"So, we will sacrifice the teleporter inventor and his assistant? Why?"

"Yes. He should have worked alongside his country and fellow countrymen."

"You mean you're doing this to get even since he didn't give you the teleporter or its blueprints."

"He made his choice, not me. Besides, I have been ordered to get the teleporter anyway I can."

"Even if it risks changing our history?"

"Come on, Garcia, how can this change our history? We will rewrite it a bit."

Garcia didn't notice Robinson's grin.

"Garcia, are you there?"

"Albert! Thank goodness! Where are you?"

"We're still in the time portal, moving slowly. We need more energy emitted into the portal to reach our destination before Karina leaves. So, can you funnel two gigahertz of energy into my system?"

Robinson grabbed Garcia's arm, stopping her from replying as he pressed the mute button on the telecom.

"Don't send any package of energy to him!"

"Why not? This will ensure their rendezvous with Karina and eventually the team's return home."

Garcia turned to Robinson as she yanked her arm from his grip.

"Wouldn't that amount of energy transfer drain the field within the time portal or the teleporter itself?"

"I am not sure, Agent Robinson. Theoretically, the teleporter would have difficulty bringing the four through the portal, but two individuals would make it without breaking a

sweat. Yet, we can figure out a way for them to get through the portal after dampening the field with 2 GHz."

"Then why take such a chance with that big energy dispersal? It's too risky; just don't transfer the energy. We're better off teleporting Karina and Wilma back to us. Wouldn't it take less energy and less risk to our timeline by bringing back both women?"

"Garcia! Are you there?" I yelled through the intercom.

Garcia flipped the switch.

"Yes, Al. Sorry about that. Agent Robinson told me I shouldn't transfer the energy."

Robinson froze with amazement that Garcia would divulge his order.

"What? Why not?"

"He believes we won't have enough energy to return all four of you."

Garcia quickly typed and sent it to me.

"I will transfer the needed GHz in 30 seconds."

"Robinson is not a scientist and is only guessing what may happen," I stated as I tried to distract Robinson from Garcia.

"Garcia, we are ready for the transfer. Be careful when you submit it. Make sure Eugene is nowhere near your console."

Robinson moved towards the mic when Garcia pointed to another near the second console. He nodded and got closer to that mic.

"Albert, I'm in charge of this mission, and I'm ordering Garcia not to transfer any energy to you or Karina, for that matter."

"Sir, you don't have any authority in acquiring the teleporter or any authority over Garcia or me, so we respectfully refuse your request."

I then added.

"Now, Garcia!"

She pressed three buttons simultaneously, suddenly sending a surge of energy from the Teleporter to Albert's TVU.

"No, Garcia!"

Robinson lunged unsuccessfully toward her. She moved over, and Robinson fell to the lab floor with a loud thud.

"Thanks, Garcia. I am inputting the new energy GHz into the coordinates reading on my device."

I quickly pressed a green button. A sudden energy surge radiated from my device into and throughout the portal, which in turn caused Corey and I to move quickly through the time portal towards our destination – Jesus Christ's Last Supper time period. Garcia shut off the intercom and looked at Robinson, who was getting up from the floor. He shook his head as he looked at the new readings on the teleporter screen, which were lower than the minimum amount for teleportation.

"I can't believe you disobey a direct order."

"Eugene, you're not my boss, and I also don't work for the FBI anymore. I don't have to obey your orders."

"You may be right about that, but remember, our main goal in this mission is to preserve our history and timeline."

"Albert and his entire team are doing just that without you meddling with your directives and waving your governmental authority and rights."

Garcia continued to monitor the teleporter's energy levels and the pair's travel through the portal in real-time. The graphs show the changing amounts of energy traveling through the portal and the traveling speed and direction for myself and Corey. Robinson brushed off any dirt from his hands and suit. He then looked over Garcia's shoulder and couldn't make heads or tails of what she was writing.

"What are you doing now?"

"It seems to be gibberish notes. If only I had my phone out to take a pic of her scribble." Robinson thought as he got closer to the console screen. He quickly laid his hand under the console without Garcia's knowledge.

"I am just writing notes of Albert's journey and more calculations for the next teleport to home for the entire team if you must know."

Garcia punched in more buttons.

"Ok, I got the message. I don't belong here. Well, keep me apprised of any new developments."

Robinson walked out of the lab confident his listening device would pick up vital information about this rescue mission.

"I will learn more about this machine and Albert's plans after they return."

"Phew! I thought he would never leave. Now let's see what Albert is up to with these new calculations Corey sent me."

Garcia opened up the link and then shook her head in amazement.

Thank You Lord

by Redemption Group

Thank you, Lord, for what You have done for me
   Thank you, Lord, for dying for me
   Thank you, Lord, for saving me
   Thank you, Lord, for all you have done for me
   I don't deserve Your love O Lord
   I don't deserve You taking the nails for me
   Lord, You freed me from God's wrath
   You saved me for all eternity
   I love You Lord, for taking upon Yourself my sins
   I love You Lord, for dying for me
   I love You Lord, for rescuing me
   Oh Jesus, You rescued me
   I know I'm saved ever since I repented and accepted You as
   my personal Savior
   I know I'm saved when You told me I'm Yours
   I know I'm saved when You gave me the Holy Spirit
   I know I'm saved for eternity
   So I thank You, my Lord, for taking it all upon Yourself
   I thank You, my Lord, for dying for me
   I thank You, my Lord, for rescuing me

Oh Lord, I love You so.

Chapter 14

August 24, 2021– 1:47 PM

"Those scientists and tech people think they can pull the wool over me. Albert, Karina, and Garcia did not realize I was an elite FBI agent, DC Police Commissioner, DC detective, and beat cop for the past 21 years. I had the highest training scores in recognizing covert activities and different methodologies of communication. Maybe they think I am just a bureaucrat since I am an FBI director. Man, that burns me, and yet, at the same time, they make me laugh. Little do they know I have at least three tricks up my sleeve."

Robinson thought as he reviewed, through his phone apps, the three bugs he planted within the lab. He got into his car and set up his phone on the vent holder. A smile crept on his face as he activated the three bugs near Garcia and the Teleporter.

"These babies should give me all the intel I need to get his machine and keep him and his team trapped in time."

As Corey and I hurdled through the time portal with the increased GHz of energy infused into the portal and my TVU, I recalled how I was not surprised by Robinson's attempt to bug my laboratory. The bugs were very active, so I told Garcia that we should relay an energy loop through an app I developed, which sent a pulse through those bugs, masking that they were active and recording every activity within the lab. We quickly found those three bugs. Decided to keep one operational while disabling the other two with minimal signals between the devices and the host receiver masking as active listening devices.

Robinson planted the first bug within my computer at my station. He put a code within the motherboard programming system of the computer. Unbeknownst to Agent Robinson, Garcia immediately discovered the bug when she scanned the computer fifteen minutes after he left the lab. The second bug was placed underneath the Teleporter's console. It lasted a few hours until its signal interfered with Garcia's transmission to the time-traveling team. The third bug was attached to Garcia herself. When Robinson and Garcia physically struggled with each other, he placed a very tiny bug upon her skin. The bug opened up quickly, inserting a thin needle into Garcia's skin along her neckline, pulling the rest of the bug under her skin. This bug was detected when Garcia used a wand scanner, which she waved over her body parts. She then relayed a signal from her phone through a link to Robinson's phone to keep the bug alive with no ability to send any important messages to Agent Robinson. Instead, it sent readouts of teleport activity and numerical readouts of the team's position within the portal or time period. Garcia destroyed the other two bugs while she kept this third one intact.

"I will have some use for this bug at a later date. I'll let him think he has gotten over me.

I can't wait to see his face once I present my findings of this bug to his superiors."

Garcia told me as much as she could while continuing her work with the Teleporter on the day it was discovered. The bug continued to transmit all activities dealing with the present mission and lab activities.

~

"Bam! Bam!"

Chairman Jones put down his gavel and turned toward the FBI Agent in charge of that operation. Robinson stood up.

"Agent Robinson, do you have any recorded intel you tried to obtain while bugging the lab and team?"

"No, Mr. Chairman. I have them sealed due to national security."

"What this group did amounts to treason towards our government, way of life, and timeline."

"Mr. Chairman, please hear them out and then decide based on the evidence presented to each of you. Also, if you're not convinced of their innocence, I will present recordings that will exonerate the entire team."

Robinson sat down without looking at the Chairman. I looked toward him, and he signaled me to continue playing the mission's recording.

~

Robinson just grinned as he drove to the Brooklyn FBI facility, the actual site for interrogating domestic terrorists in the tri-state area, totally unaware of the future demise of his bugs. He pulled up to the gated entrance and flashed his microchipped badge over a plated screen, which opened the gate. He drove through unto he reached Lot # 3. Robinson entered a nondescript building, which looked like a sizeable concrete cinder box, and went through several security checks until he entered Interrogation Block A. He snickered as he signed in for Room 007.

"If only James Bond could assist me with this interrogation."

The sector guard buzzed Robinson into a room with one large table and two wooden chairs. The metallic walls reflected the coldness within the room even though it was steaming hot throughout the building. He proceeded to open his satchel and took out a memo pad, recorder, and a small video camera. Robinson didn't bother to look at the prisoner wearing grey prison jumpers, even for one second. He then clicked both electronic devices on and said,

"Today is August 24th, 2021, at 1:57 pm. Mr. Gary McGee is present for his first interrogation on domestic crimes to change specific historical events in the United States

of America. This crime can kill thousands or destroy our country as we know it. Mr. McGee, what do you say about these charges?"

McGee's sweat rolled from his forehead to brow as he raised his head and looked dead into Robinson's eyes.

"You forgot the theft of classified tech information and blueprints."

Robinson grinned.

"Right, tech espionage."

He sat across McGee, who extended his fingers in a manner for a handshake while handcuffed to the interrogation table. Robinson's mouth creased slightly to reveal a bigger smile.

"Do you have anything to say about these charges?"

"No. They are correct for now."

"What do you mean by that?"

McGee didn't respond.

"Look, McGee; you know how this plays out since you were an agent a few years ago."

"Yeah, a few rounds of rope de rope until someone takes the first hit. Well, it ain't going to be me, Robinson."

"I have one more question before I leave."

"Ok, shoot."

"How did you disturb the time portal?"

"Oh, that. Mr. Robinson, do you know how an earthquake works?"

"I think so."

"Well, think of the time portal disturbance in that way – a portal quake, which I like to call it."

McGee smiled with pride in thinking up the term.

"Ok, how did you develop this portal quake?"

Robinson didn't get an answer and was not surprised by McGee's nonresponsive attitude. He packed his electronic items and left the room in a huff.

"Just great, no true answer to my questions. I wonder if Garcia can understand McGee's analogy and solve the portal problem."

He got into his car, leaving the site with nothing to show. He wanted the smoking gun but only had more questions about the mission. He drove quickly through the streets of Manhattan to reach my lab.

Chapter 15

28 AD

"Blip!"

Two bodies fell onto two separate areas which were near each other. The first body landed on a large pile of hay or straw, while the second fell within a large trough filled with water. Each man slowly rose from their landing spot due to the impact of their fall. I looked around as I climbed from the hay and tried to locate Corey while understanding their surroundings.

"Hey Corey, are you ok?"

Corey pulled himself out of the trough and shook the water from his hair and body, almost like a dog would shake excess water after a bath. I smiled and tried to hold back from laughing, but unsuccessfully.

"Ha...Ha...Ha! Are you ok, Corey?"

"Yeah, real funny, Al. I wish the time portal led us to different landing spots."

"Sorry I laughed, Corey, but it was hilarious. As for the portal, we cannot control when, how, or where it releases us into time."

"Maybe we can manipulate it with certain calculations, bringing us to safe landing sites."

"I'll look into it once we get back home. Seriously, are you ok?"

"Yeah, I'm fine. No broken bones, just wet and embarrassed."

I took my large towel from my satchel and gave it to him.

"I'm relieved you're ok. I hope this towel will do the trick."

Corey took it and vigorously dried himself. I took out and turned on my TVU and two other gadgets. I wasn't sure where we landed, and I could not pinpoint the time period by examining the buildings in the area. There were not many of them. I also noticed no trace evidence of pollution in the air.

"Hey Al, where are we?"

"I'm not sure, but we can no longer stay here. We need to get back to our time period."

Corey was about to ask another question when a loud commotion from the crowd momentarily stopped him. I also noticed that the crowd was praising and condemning someone simultaneously. The crowd was wearing certain clothes, which reminded me of movies and shows depicting the time of Jesus.

"Let's check out what the ruckus is all about."

"Hold on Al, I thought we shouldn't get involved with historical events?"

"Yes, I did say that, but there seems to be a rally around a man. There is no way we can change this event by observing it."

"I hope you're right."

We joined the crowd, which flowed towards a medium-sized stone building. We were able to enter without an incident. The people were so engrossed with the man they were railing that they didn't even notice us or our 1860s costumes. Once inside, the people settled down. I looked around to find the town's women standing on the balcony while the men were on the main sanctuary of the building.

"Jesus will read from the book of Isaiah."

I froze as my eyes searched within the crowd and found Jesus.

"Am I dreaming? Did he say Jesus, like the Savior of the world? You know the Son of God."

"Yes, he did. Let's see what transpires from this event."

Jesus walked up to the podium. And the scroll of Isaiah the prophet was handed to Him. And He unrolled the scroll and found the place where it was written:

"The Spirit of the Lord is upon Me,

Because He anointed Me to bring good news to the poor.
He has sent Me to proclaim release to captives,
And recovery of sight to the blind,
To set free those who are oppressed,
To proclaim the favorable year of the Lord."

And He rolled up the scroll, gave it back to the attendant, and sat down; the eyes of all the people in the synagogue were intently directed at Him.

"That's it? Jesus is just going to sit there?"

"Hold on Corey. He will say something that may shock you."

Now He began to say to them,

"Today this Scripture has been fulfilled in your hearing."

And all the people were speaking well of Him, and admiring the gracious words which were coming from His lips, and yet they were saying,

"Is this not Joseph's son?"

"Wow! He is bold in claiming that the prophecy has been fulfilled. I think they will stone Him and His disciples, Al."

"You may be right, but He couldn't contain His boldness. He just proclaimed that He is the Messiah."

And He said to them,

"No doubt you will quote this proverb to Me: 'Physician, heal yourself! All the miracles that we heard were done in Capernaum, do here in your hometown as well.'"

But He said,

"Truly I say to you, no prophet is welcome in his hometown. But I say to you in truth, there were many widows in Israel in the days of Elijah when the sky was shut up for three years and six months, when a severe famine came over all the land; and yet Elijah was sent to none of them, but only to Zarephath, in the land of Sidon, to a woman who was a widow. And there were many with leprosy in Israel in the time of Elisha the prophet, and none of them was cleansed, but only Naaman the Syrian."

"What was He trying to tell the people with these past prophets?"

"Jesus emphasizes that selected people are healed based on their growing faith, and God will grant salvation, healing, and grace upon the Gentiles."

And all the people in the synagogue were filled with rage as they heard these things; and they got up and drove Him out of the city and brought Him to the crest of the hill on which their city had been built so that they could throw Him down from the cliff.

"How can we stop them from killing Jesus?"

"They won't kill Him. God will not permit His death because it was not His time."

But He passed through their midst and went on His way.

"Buzz!"

"Yes, Garcia, what's our travel status to Karina and Wilma? Did you record the images along the portal walls? Please review them and let us know what we are dealing with."

"No problem. You will be the first to know."

"Hey Al, do you know what they mean?"

"No, I don't. How about you Corey?"

"I have no idea at all?"

Garcia signed out to examine those images. After three minutes, she signaled me.

"Buzz!"

"Hey Garcia, any news over there?

"Yes, the appearances of those images may have a connection to ripples within the time continuum."

"Ok? Well, can we get to Karina and Wilma with the existence of those ripples?"

"Yes Al, but as you know, those ripples may cause us to be a bit off with our teleport calculations, and we may not enter the desire time period."

"We still need to follow our plan."

"Corey, you're right. So Garcia, are you ready to teleport us to Karina and Wilma?"

"Yes. Here we go."

"Zip!"

We immediately dematerialized from the same cliff where the crowd tried to push Jesus off. Also, no one noticed our disappearance.

Chapter 16

November 19, 1863 – 3:15 PM

The energy force of the time portal and the newly inputted energy from Garcia hurdled us quickly through that shimmery tunnel. They made us unconscious due to their great force when we entered the plotted time period. I slowly opened my eyes and witnessed blurry blotches.

"Was this all a dream?"

I carefully sat up, trying to prevent dizziness, and looked around to find myself on a field with many people gathering across a dusty road. The sky was overcast, yet there was not one threatening cloud. I tried to move my right leg, but there was some heaviness as if a log or something similar laid upon it. I looked at my leg to find it trapped by Corey's leg.

"Well, I'm sure it's not a dream since Corey's weighty leg has impeded my leg. Now, where are we? This scene doesn't look like ancient Israel."

Corey moved a little bit. I carefully nudged him.

"Hey Corey, get up. We need to find some cover and find out where we landed."

"Huh? Oh, ok Al. I feel a bit numb."

Corey slowly got up. We walked over to a group of bushes and trees near a large gathering in a tremendous open field. We got out our devices to contact Garcia and scan the region for location and time.

"Hey Garcia, can you read me?"

Only static replied. I lowered the volume of my TVU to ensure no one noticed my device. Corey started his scanning procedure to triangulate our time period position.

"Great! Now we are blind, deaf, and dumb on where we landed. Corey, what have you found out so far?"

"If my chromometer is correct, we entered November 19, 1863. My device is also indicating that we're in Gettysburg."

"Now I wish Karina is here. She would know exactly what event is occurring on this date."

"Hold on, Al. I'll get that in a few seconds.... well, in a few minutes since my device was temporarily turned off when we arrived and would take some time to search for that information."

"Corey, don't worry. We have time to find out. More importantly, we must find out how to get to Karina and Wilma before the opportune rendezvous time frame closes."

While searching for our location, I took some time to observe the weather, which was cloudy with a hint of rain in the air; maybe it was morning dew. We weren't sure. A crowd grew quickly upon a freshly cut, expansive field, which may have signaled a big event was about to happen. Several horse-drawn buggies appeared, revealing what seemed to contain some dignitaries of the time period.

"Man, what's going on over here, Al?"

"I don't know Corey, but look at that buggy with the military escort. Doesn't it look familiar?"

"Yes, that's Lincoln buggy."

"Right! Hold on, didn't you say that we're in Gettysburg?"

"That's right; why?"

"Corey, this is the memorial site or cemetery for the Battle of Gettysburg."

"Ok?"

"This is where and when Lincoln delivered his famous short speech, the Gettysburg Address."

"Bing!"

Corey looked at his device: **'November 19, 1863 – Gettysburg Address'**.

"Your device confirms it, right?"

"Yes sir, but do you think we can get out of here real soon?"

"We must, or we will be stuck in this time frame forever. Garcia hasn't answered my radio message or text. Either we are not sending any signal to her, or the time portal is preventing our transmission."

"What are we going to do?"

"Well, for now, let's witness history. We can't do anything right now since our devices are rebooting."

"You got a point Al."

We walked over to the crowd, waiting patiently for the orators to arrive at this organized ceremony. Lincoln exited his buggy and walked up to the crowd, which parted a seam for him to transverse to its epicenter. I signaled Corey to lower the volume of his device so it wouldn't interrupt the proceedings and cause a blip in history. He nodded and complied quickly. As Lincoln walked through the crowd, a cheer rippled among it while some people murmured disappointment at Lincoln's appearance. Within minutes, the crowd settled down. It was a day of ceremonial remembrance for the fallen in the Battle of Gettysburg. One speaker took two hours to complete his speech, and it was Edward Everett. During his speech, I continued trying to contact Garcia with no success.

"Al, how much time do we have to rendezvous with Karina and Wilma and then return to our time period?"

"From what I got from Garcia, along with the specs of the time portal and its energy, we have approximately thirty-three minutes once we reach Karina and Wilma."

"So, there is no chance for the portal door to close before we get to them?"

"Theoretically, no."

Corey and I smiled briefly when we realized Everett's speech was ending.

"That's a relief. Hey Corey, I thought he would talk for another hour."

"Yeah, I thought so too."

Everyone clapped, and after a small band with violins, saxophones, guitars, and banjos concluded, the next speaker was Abraham Lincoln. He got up, held a small piece of paper, and paused as he looked at it carefully. A crackling noise and a distant voice emanated from my TVU.

"Hey Albert, Corey! Is there anyone out there?"

I quickly fumbled through my bag until I got my device.

"Hola Garcia. How are you?"

"I'm fine. How about you and Corey?"

"We are good."

"OK, enough with the pleasantries. Garcia, how long do we have until the portal door closes after gathering Wilma and my Karina?"

"You have at least two to three hours to return to the portal and reach Karina. Once you reach her, you have thirty-three minutes to reenter the other portal and return home."

"Garcia, do you have all the specs for our entry into the portal?"

"No, Al. I am still figuring out what caused your sudden trips. I'll get back to you when I have the right specs and coding to prevent any more unexpected stops to another time period."

Corey aggressively took my device and spoke loudly into it.

"Now we have to hang out in this cemetery for the next few hours while we wait for you to figure out an answer to our dilemma, and while you do that, the portal will close, preventing us from reentry and our return home!"

I was shocked by Corey's outburst, but no one even bothered to look our way. I took my device from him and said,

"Corey, remember those hours in a time period are minutes in our present time period. So, the two to three hours in your time event are anywhere from two to three minutes or twenty to thirty minutes in our present time period, depending on the increment time measurements and time distance between our present time and the time period you entered."

"Yeah, I know Al, but I want to get back to my wife, hug her, and be assured that our time period is safe and secure from any terrorist act."

"Don't worry Corey. I'll return with the appropriate specs for your rendezvous point with Karina and Wilma."

"Thanks, Garcia. I'm sorry if I seemed untrustworthy with your data," Corey said with some remorse.

"Oh, come on Corey, if I were there with you, I would react the same way. Don't worry; I will get the needed calculations for your travel through the portal in time. Both of you will get it in a few minutes. Garcia out!"

"You got it, Garcia!"

Corey lowered his head in shame. I closed the communique on my TVU and put it in my satchel.

Abraham Lincoln read the first line of his speech,

"Four score and seven years ago our fathers brought forth on this continent, a new nation, conceived in Liberty and dedicated to the proposition that all men are created equal."

I tried to bring Corey out of his funk dealing with our situation.

"It's incredible that we can witness this historical event."

"Yeah, it is, but I really want to get home."

"I hear you buddy, and believe me, I want the same thing, but we need to wait for Garcia's research on our situation."

"Bing!"

I quickly grabbed my device as my heart yelped in joy.

"Now I can get back with Karina," I thought.

"Hey Garcia, what's the update?"

"Honey, it's me, Karina."

"What? You can reach me?"

"Yes, I've been trying for the past half hour."

"I'm so glad to hear your voice, Sweetie."

"What's the deal, Al? Are you still at the Confederate White House? We have been waiting for a while, and you should have been here already."

"Yeah, I know. The time portal or another force caused us to enter a Biblical event and ...."

"Which Biblical event?"

"Oh, when Jesus read from the Book of Isaiah stating the day of the Lord in which the blind recover their sight, the poor are rescued, etc. After He read that passage, Jesus

proclaimed that the scripture has been fulfilled."

"Wow! I wish I were there."

"No Karina, you would have witnessed the crowd trying to force Jesus off a cliff."

"Really? So, are you still there?"

"No, we're at a cemetery on November 19, 1863."

"Are you kidding me? The Gettysburg Address!"

"Yep, and Lincoln is giving it right now. Take a listen."

I discreetly pointed my device toward Lincoln.

"But, in a larger sense, we can not dedicate – we can not consecrate – we can not hallow – this ground," Lincoln continued.

"I wish I could witness such a momentous event."

"I know Sweetie, but it was just by chance that we're here to witness this unfolding history."

"Honey, is it by chance, or did God allow you to be there for a greater purpose?"

"What do you mean?"

"Listen to Lincoln's words and heed the importance of those words. God does not do chance or accidents. You being there is God-driven."

"Really? I hope He gives me a sign to explain why I am here."

"He will Honey. So, when will you be here? I can't wait to get back home."

"Kari, we will be there to rendezvous with you within an hour or so."

"Good. We will continue to wait in hiding. Just signal when you're on your way to us."

"I will Sweet e. Garcia will get back to me with the proper specs and calculations to get back home."

"I can't wait."

"Me too. I'll see you soon. Albert out!"

"– that we here highly resolve that these dead shall not have died in vain – that this nation, under God, shall have a new birth of freedom – and that government of the

people, by the people, for the people, shall not perish from the earth," Lincoln concluded his speech.

"This speech mirrored the founding fathers' principles and their foundational belief in God, or at that time, they called it – Providence. I must live like this, looking towards

God and pointing to Him with everything I say and do. Unfortunately, I can't help myself from doing the opposite with my personal mission. I need to tell Kari everything

about this issue."

I thought about my lack of dependence on God. Corey turned towards me.

"Now, that was a speech. If only people from our time period could hear it."

"Especially our youth."

"Beep!"

"Yes Garcia?"

"Let's get you guys back on track. I'll explain what happened later on. We don't have enough time to discuss it unless you want to miss your rendezvous point and your return trip home."

"Not necessary; let's start the sequence."

"10, 9, 8, 7, 6, 5, 4, 3, 2, 1."

"Zap!"

Corey and I entered the correct portal for Karina and Wilma. I took my device out, pressed three buttons, and texted.

"I hope you get this signal before we get to you, Sweetie. We are on our way to you!"

Chapter 17

August 24, 2021– 2:05 PM

Robinson returned to the lab after interrogating McGee. His men had completed fixing the laboratory door, and he noticed a skeleton crew within and around the lab. He brought his Apple iPad to show a portion of the interrogation to Garcia, hoping to get her to transmit it to me through the Teleporter.

"Garcia, you need to see this."

Robinson typed in the security code to open his iPad.

"Sure, as long as it helps solve our time portal problem."

Garcia blanked out her computer screen because she didn't trust Robinson and needed to secure any data, intel, or materials dealing with the Teleporter from him and his agents. She observed close to fifteen minutes of the rambling from McGee's mouth. Garcia shrugged, returned to her computer, turned on its monitor, and continued collecting detailed data.

"I know it's not much, but do you believe him?"

"You need to give me his TVU and any other gadgets he possessed and possibly used during his rogue mission."

Garcia insisted as she ignored his question.

"Why?"

"His gadgets, especially his Time Viewer Unit, may shed some light on what has happened to the time portal and whether he is the cause of it."

"I thought you may say that."

Robinson pulled McGee's device out of his black satchel.

"Great job Eugene!"

"Will you be able to retrieve anything from this device?"

"I hope so."

Garcia examined the machine.

"This is an older version, in fact, the prototype. How did he get his hands on this model? There is no way he got any blueprints for this version since there were none sketched out by Al or anyone else on the team."

"Do you need any of my tech people to help you?"

"No, I got this."

Garcia attached McGee's device through a USB port into Karina's computer. She used the TVU program to retrieve all records and codes from his device. It took three minutes to populate the computer screen with coded number sequences that appeared randomly and incomprehensible to anyone except for Garcia, Corey, and myself. Robinson got closer to the computer screen.

"I can't make anything from those mess of numbers."

"Don't you worry, Mr. Robinson; I can break this code and get the answer you need, but it will take at minimum three months."

"Really? Man, I was hoping for a quick solution for this time portal issue."

Garcia shut off the computer screen without Robinson realizing it.

"Hey? Did the computer break down?"

Robinson slaps the computer and then its screen a couple of times. Garcia waved at him to stop. He did as she slapped her forehead in shock.

"It's ok. I will see what's the problem with the computer. Maybe the program has a virus within the code and causes the computer to shut down. I'll look into it."

"Ok, you got it, Garcia. Before I arrived, I retrieved all videos McGee had recorded before he embarked on his reckless mission and videos during that mission."

"I will see if I can get any intel from those videos the old-fashioned way."

Robinson walked out of the lab.

"Thanks for the device and the videos, Eugene."

A few minutes after Robinson left the laboratory, Garcia put on the computer screen and took pictures of the code. She fed the information into a code breaker program installed on Karina's computer.

"Now, let's see what's giving the portal indigestion."

Chapter 18

30 AD

"Blip!"

We landed along a wide, long road. As we dusted ourselves, we looked around for any buildings or landmarks. Instead, we found Jesus walking with His disciples toward a large city.

"I believe that's Jesus with His disciples heading towards Jerusalem."

"How are you so sure, Al?"

"Well, let me check my TVU and Time Locator."

Instantly, both devices indicated,

"30 AD – Jesus' Triumphal Entry into Jerusalem".

I showed it to Corey.

"Should we join them?"

"Let's just follow them, but not so close."

We walked about five to seven feet behind Jesus and his followers. He looked back at us and smiled.

"Albert, it's nice of you to join us."

I shook my head, looked around, and then at Jesus.

"Did you hear that?"

"Hear what, Al?"

"Never mind, I must be imagining things or daydreaming events."

I was the only one who could hear the Lord's audible voice.

"Albert, you can lean on me with your mess, and I will comfort you. Coach Hood's death will not change anything within your heart and soul. You need to surrender the anguish caused by Coach Hood and ask Me to fix it."

"How can You fix it? It's an event I cannot change. You're a gentleman, which means You will not try to fix it since that awful event is etched into the stones of time."

Walking along that dusty road, I whispered to Jesus like I was praying to Him. There was silence for the next three miles, during which we saw the following:

He sent two of His disciples, and said to them,

"Go into the village opposite you, and immediately as you enter it you will find a colt tied there, on which no one has ever sat; untie it and bring it here. And if anyone says to you, 'Why are you doing this?' say, 'The Lord has need of it'; and immediately he will send it back here."

They went away for a few minutes, anywhere from twenty to forty minutes, and then brought the colt to Jesus and put their cloaks on it; and He sat on it. And many people spread their cloaks on the road, and others spread leafy branches they had cut from palm trees. And those who went in front and those who followed were shouting:

"Hosanna!

Blessed is He who comes in the name of the Lord;

Blessed is the coming kingdom of our father David;

Hosanna in the highest!"

And Jesus entered Jerusalem and came into the temple area; and after looking around at everything, He left for Bethany with the twelve since it was already late. Corey and I went back to the heart of Jerusalem.

"That was some entry into Jerusalem. Does that mean He is the Messiah, and He wants everyone to know?"

"Yes Corey, He didn't deny their shouts of joy proclaiming Jesus as Messiah and Lord."

"Really?"

I took out my iPhone, pressed the Study Bible app, and scrolled to a particular reading.

"Yes, in fact, the Word stated the following in Matthew 21:10-11:

When He had entered Jerusalem, all the city was stirred, saying, "Who is this?"

And the crowds were saying, "This is Jesus the prophet, from Nazareth in Galilee."

"What else does the Bible say?"

"In Luke 19: 37b – 40 it states:

The whole crowd of the disciples began to praise God joyfully with a loud voice for all the miracles which they had seen, shouting:

"Blessed is the King, the One who comes in the name of the Lord;

Peace in heaven and glory in the highest!"

And yet some of the Pharisees in the crowd said to Him,

"Teacher, rebuke Your disciples!"

Jesus replied,

"I tell you, if these stop speaking, the stones will cry out!"

"With all of this evidence, why couldn't the Pharisees accept Jesus as the Son of God? They should have at least accepted the miracles."

"They have sins which they haven't repented. Their sin dealt with pride, prestige, and money."

"Wow! This means God doesn't mince with His words, and we need to heed them."

We went back to the heart of Jerusalem after Jesus left for Bethany.

"Crackle! Crackle!"

"Hey Corey, get ready; we are about to get sucked back into the time portal."

"Really? I can't believe it. What's triggering the sudden teleportation to other time periods?"

"I guess what McGee did in the 1860s within the Confederate White House."

"Zap!"

Jesus looked back at where we were standing and saw nothing. He smiled and then continued walking with His disciples to Bethany.

Chapter 19

30 AD

"Bleep!"

We softly landed in a poorly lit room, with several torches inserted into slots along the room's four walls. We leaned against a wall to regain our balance and then moved behind a stone pillar as we heard a commotion on the other side of the room. We observed an assembly of men speaking feverishly with each other, more like debating about something or someone, and then suddenly, guards brought a Man bound by shackles into the room. I saw He was bloodied, as if beaten by the very men pushing Him into the room. My heart grieved for Him because the Man was Jesus Christ.

"Oh no!"

"What is it, Al?"

"This is the secret trial the Sanhedrin performed to sentence Jesus to death."

"Really? No one stopped them?"

"The Chief Priest had many supporters who didn't mind this illegal trial."

"Was it really illegal?"

"Yes, based on Jewish law, but the Pharisees had their own agenda."

We moved to a corner of that room so I could use the Detector. I fed it with the calculations we used for our recent travel through the time portal and from what time period we came from. The purpose of this machine was not only to give us how and why we got here but also to give two other facts. First, it gave us the exact historical event we entered, and second, it gave us the appropriate solution to our portal problem. It stated,

"30 AD Sanhedrin Council Room, Council members condemn Jesus".

Now the chief priests and the entire Council were trying to obtain testimony against Jesus to put Him to death, and they were not finding any. Many people gave false testimony against Him, so their testimonies were inconsistent.

"We heard Him say, 'I will destroy this temple that was made by hands, and in three days. I will build another, made without hands.'"

And not even in this respect was their testimony consistent.

"It's incredible those people lied."

"Corey, many of them were paid off by the Pharisees so that they could condemn Jesus, but a few Pharisees became followers of Jesus. They were witnesses to many false claims and refuted their testimony."

"Thank God they did."

And then the high priest stood up and came forward and questioned Jesus, saying,

"Do You not offer any answer for what these men are testifying against You?"

But He kept silent and did not offer any answer. Again the high priest was questioning Him and said to Him,

"Are You the Christ, the Son of the Blessed One?"

And Jesus said,

"I am; and you shall see the Son of Man sitting at the right hand of power, and coming with the clouds of heaven."

Tearing his clothes, the high priest said,

"What further need do we have of witnesses? You have heard the blasphemy; how does it seem to you?"

"Wow! The high priest just went nuts. Man, he wants Jesus out of the way."

"Yes, Jesus changed everything about our relationship with God."

"So this is how He changed our relationship with God; by dying for us?"

"Jesus showed us how to live by seeking God and laying our cares upon Him. Jesus, Who is sinless, also took upon Himself the wrath we are supposed to receive from Father God because of our sin."

"Wow! That is incredible! He did that for me?"

"Yes, He did. Now let's see how the Council votes."

And they all condemned Him as deserving of death. And some began to spit on Him, and to blindfold Him, and to beat Him with their fists and say to Him,

"Prophesy!"

Then the officers took custody of Him and slapped Him in the face.

"Hey guys, can you hear me? Anyone there?"

"Hola Garcia. We are alive and kicking, just a bit missing."

"Funny, Al. Are you ready for another attempt at the present?"

"Ready or not, Garcia, start the process."

In twenty-one seconds, we went through another time portal.

"Zap!"

I just hoped we would reach Karina and Wilma in time for us to return home. Despite several delays, we could teleport with no significant issues.

Chapter 20

July 12, 1864 – 9:30 AM

A blinding light flashed near a huge building made of either granite or marble. Two bodies fell from the sky and landed near the building.

"Thud!"

"Man, we need to have some eye in the sky to show where we may land from exiting the time portal. Maybe I can figure out how to control our entry into a time period to ensure a safe entrance. Amazingly, not one of us has gotten any serious injuries from our unusual entry into different time periods."

I shook my head with that thought as I slowly got up. Corey and I took a few minutes to recover from our rubber band teleport into this unknown time event. We looked around to get our bearings of when we entered besides where.

"Al, is that what I think it is?"

Corey pointed to a partially constructed building with a large rotunda.

"Yes Corey, it's the rotunda of the Capital building, partially completed in its mid-construction, and it looks like we got sideswiped into another time period."

We walked over to a row of trees and hid to examine our entry time period. Corey used his TVU to trace the energy pattern from the point of our time portal entry to our exact position in terms of date and location. I saw a young lady with her hand holding onto a man's arm while walking on a path near our location. The couple was wearing mid-1800s clothing. I was relieved that we still had on our Union uniforms.

"Corey, you don't have to search the data banks for our event period. It's the 1860s due to the style of clothes everyone is wearing. Confederates are approaching from many boats along the shore. This doesn't look good."

I pointed to several boats as I looked through my field glasses, which may have numbered from 10 to 20 boats, about 600 to 900 feet away,

"We need to take cover, Al."

"No worries. These trees, the benches, and the people have given us enough cover. Anyway, I believe they are going to head over to the rotunda. Our main concern is getting back to our teammates and home."

Corey surveyed the area.

"You're right, Al, but I want to know the exact date. This will tell us what important event we shouldn't disturb."

"Bing!"

Corey looked at his TVU's screen, which showed,

"July 12, 1864, Washington, DC, near the Potomac River".

Corey showed me what appeared on his device's screen. I end up asking Corey a question, not expecting an answer.

"What could be the significance of this date and why here? How does this area relate to the Civil War?"

I don't remember any other questions I might have asked.

"I am not sure. Maybe the historical data in our TVUs can provide the significance to this time event."

Corey typed in the date and the circumstances, like the incomplete Capital building, to get the relevant information.

"Look Corey, we need to stay hidden until either Garcia or I find a way to get us back into the portal, directly linking us to Karina and Wilma."

"Do you believe we can get back to our team and return home on time?"

Corey stared at me while waiting for any answer I could possibly give. I know Corey will pick up any cues from my answer to see whether I am lying. This was the only answer I was able to give.

"As long as we enter the portal within seven to fourteen minutes and go through it with the normal speed energy input, we should get home within the time frame we calculated earlier."

"I wonder if this answer satisfied Corey. On top of that, I can't believe McGee's action towards the portal's energy field has caused this much instability."

"Al, this is our third or fourth detour. If we continue to have these portal interruptions or detours, we may not reach Karina and Wilma on time, let alone get home at all."

"I know. It's incredible how McGee did this. Robinson must find out what he did and how we can fix it. In the meantime, we need to connect with Garcia and figure out how to get to the Last Supper Event."

"I'm on it, boss."

"Good. I'll get some calculations going while you survey the area."

I left Corey behind three rows of trees and walked at least thirty to forty feet from him. I made sure that those Confederate troops could not detach my presence. To my right was the Capitol building with an incomplete dome. The pristine, clean look was breathtaking, and then I snapped myself back to our present situation – temporarily stuck in 1864. I took out my Time Viewer Unit and looked at the environmental readings dealing with certain chemical compounds for that region. The screen on my device read 49% gunpowder and 51% of other typical chemicals in 1864 air. I then pressed a yellow button on my device to administer an infrared scan of the region. I noticed those Confederate troops landing near the cobble path I was walking, but away from my present position and Corey's. Further up the river, I saw Union troops gathering supplies and ammunition from one of their ships. I started walking towards an area adjacent to the ship but suddenly stopped when I saw Abraham Lincoln talking to a couple of officers near that ship.

"I can't believe the President is here exposed in broad daylight with his troops."

"Ding!" I answered my TVU com, "Yes Corey?"

"Hey Al, I got Garcia on channel 12, and she is unhappy."

"Thanks, Corey."

I turned the knob to the appropriate channel.

"Hey Garcia, what's up?"

"Al, what's going on with the portal? I thought you solved this problem. If you guys don't get to the Last Supper event within twenty-one minutes, then make either the 1800s or 33 AD your home forever."

"Are you done, Garcia?"

"Yes, I believe so."

"Good. Let's start talking about a more pressing issue, like how we can get through a time portal to our desired destination without further detours."

"Do you have an idea, Al?"

"In fact, I do, and it will need some interesting engineering on our part to make it through the portal. I'm sending my calculations to you right now. Please tell me what you think. In the meantime, we'll sit tight."

"Ok Al, I read you loud and clear. I'll get back to you as soon as I clear these calculations. Garcia out!"

"Good, Albert out!"

I rendezvous with Corey, and we high-tailed it to Lincoln's camp near the Union ship. Once we got there, we walked up to Lincoln.

"Hello, Mr. President, my name is Albert, and this is Corey. We're honored to shake your hand."

"Good day, gentlemen."

Lincoln reached out to shake my hand when I saw a flicker of light shining from some bushes off to my right side. I quickly grabbed Lincoln's hand and pulled him down. A shot rang out, which narrowly missed Lincoln.

"Are you alright, Mr. President?"

"Yes, I am ok, soldier. Thank you."

Lincoln got up slowly as he brushed off any dirt from his suit.

"No problem, sir. Corey and I will find out where that shot came from, Mr. President."

"Yes, do so and be careful, gentlemen."

We nodded. After the missed shot, the Union soldiers along that pier pulled into formation and protected the President from other attempts on his life. Corey and I ran from there to the rows of trees and further down the shore. We found no one in that area except burnt gunpowder and the paper casing for the gunpowder. I picked up the casing and some of the gunpowder.

"The powder is still warm."

"Hey Al, do you think we're changing history?"

"No. I remembered reading about this event. We didn't change anything. Instead, we became part of it, and hopefully, our names will not appear in the history books dealing with this event."

"So that's ok?"

"As long as we don't change the overall event, it's ok."

"Buzz!"

I grabbed my device.

"Yes, Garcia?"

"Your calculations are dead on, and we can use them now. Are you guys ready?"

"Yeah, let's do this. I just want to get home," Corey said.

Garcia started the countdown.

"10, 9, 8, 7."

"Are we heading to Karina or straight home?"

I just wanted to make sure we're going straight to Karina.

"No worries Al, I know you want to be with her. I am making sure you're heading to her."

"Thanks, Garcia."

"6, 5, 4,"

"Garcia, will we make it home on time?" Corey said.

"Yes Corey. You guys should make it according to Al's calculations."

"And if they are correct, we should gain more time to the rendezvous spot and turn around for our trip back home," I announced as I winked at Corey.

"3, 2, 1."

"Zap!"

Chapter 21

33 AD

"Ding!"

Karina picked up her device, looked at its screen, and found the following:

"I hope you get this message before we get to you, Sweetie."

She smiled and typed:

"I got it, honey. I will start the teleport sequence right now."

Karina pressed the interface buttons on the TVU's screen, revealing the sequence that Garcia and I sent earlier. The portal opened up briefly as the power within her device revved up, and just like snapping your fingers, the portal energy and the TVU energy source diminished quickly to zero.

"Oh no! What happened?"

Karina repeatedly inputted the same buttons, resulting in no change at all. Wilma saw Karina punch her Time Viewer Unit after failing to open the portal for the third time, "Aye!"

She approached Karina.

"I presume you can't open the portal?"

"We don't have enough power to open the time portal, let alone get out of this time period altogether."

"What? I did a diagnostic of our TVUs a few minutes ago, and the energy for both units was at their optimum level."

"Yes, I saw the same thing. When I started my input sequence, the energy levels were correct for time travel, but instantly, those levels decreased by more than 50%. This means we cannot even open a hole through the time portal or, as Al would put it, any section of the time field."

Karina quickly did a TVU diagnostic and rechecked the readings I sent earlier.

"What is causing the drainage? I thought Garcia fixed those energy issues since Albert and Corey could reenter the portal and move forward toward us."

"I thought so, but it seems something, or someone is sucking the energy right out of the time continuum, and I have no idea what's causing it. I am sure Al or Garcia has a theory about this new development. If anyone can find the answer to this puzzle, they can."

"Isn't Albert's arrival to this time period imminent?"

"Yes. He should have been here five minutes ago from their 1864 stopover."

A sudden flash appeared a few feet from them within seconds of Karina saying those words. Albert and Corey entered the 33 AD scene with not much physical grace. They tumbled together against a horse-drawn cart. Karina ran towards her husband and hugged him firmly.

"What took you so long?"

"Sweetie, besides being sidetracked twice in the 1800s and popping into 28 AD and 30 AD, we were stuck within the portal again, and I had to change the energy field parameters to get here."

She took Albert and Corey back to her hiding spot. Both men greeted Wilma with a hug.

"That explains it, Al."

"Explains what, Karina?"

"Corey, we had a power outage when Karina tried to start the sequence for our entrance into the portal for our return home."

"Is that right, Kari?" I spoke.

"Yes Al, and I don't know how to fix it."

"Let's put our heads together with Garcia and try to solve this problem."

I took out my TVU.

"Garcia, are you there?"

No answer. I brought my device closer to my mouth as if that would make my transmission clearer.

"Garcia?"

I looked at the specs within my TVU and found that my device was not recharging.

"Guys, we may have a problem with our devices. Please check your device's energy level and your battery's settings."

I rubbed my forehead as the stress level of this mission had significantly increased. Karina, Corey, and Wilma tried to put on their devices with just a tiny flicker of energy in each of them. For fifteen to twenty minutes, ideas flew between us in the hopes of reaching a solution. Then suddenly, Wilma came up with a prominent and brilliant idea.

"Can we harness and divert all of the energy from these devices into one device and reconnect with the teleporter to enter the time portal?"

Corey and I looked at each other. He shrugged his shoulders as I nodded.

"Make it so with my TVU. What do we have to lose?"

"Well Honey, we can lose one big thing: our time-related existence to our personal history."

"Excuse me, my friends; I couldn't help noticing all of you huddled together. Can I offer you a meal upstairs? We have enough room for you to join us."

An Israelite suddenly appeared to us and spoke those kind words. Karina took one step backward as Corey and Wilma quickly hid their devices while I looked at the Man and realized it was Jesus.

"Yes, we would like to join you, my Lord. My name is Albert, and these are Karina, my wife, Corey, and Wilma, our friends."

"I know. Follow me. You can eat a meal and rest with us before returning home to your time period."

I was stunned and couldn't walk for a moment. Karina nudged me so we could follow Him.

"Jesus, are you sure you want us to join you and your disciples?"

I asked as we reached the building where He was staying.

"Albert, it is no problem. We have enough room; besides, you all look tired and hungry. We have more than enough food for you and my friends. Also, staying with us briefly will not disturb the time continuum."

Jesus looked back at me and smiled. I couldn't help myself from smiling right back at Him. I also gave Him a thumbs-up. Yeah, I know; it was a cheesy response. We entered the building and walked up a flight of stairs. Once at the top of those stairs, the room opened to a vast area with a large table on one side. A few disciples got up from their reclined position at the table and went to a serving table to replenish their empty plates. On the other side was another table with large dishes of food and beverages. Under the table were a large basin and jug with several folded clothes and towels. Jesus directed us to sit near the setup table while He joined His disciples.

"Al, are you sure it's okay that we are here? Wouldn't our presence change history?"

"Wilma, it's ok. We are just four of many in this room during the Last Supper. As long we don't interfere with the proceedings of this event, we are fine."

They sat down, and the ladies in the room served the weary, hungry time travelers.

Chapter 22

33 AD

The room was lit in different corners, which gave it a hazy, shadowy environment. Whenever anyone got up and walked through the room, their shadows changed shapes from one end to another. Jesus sat down among His disciples and spoke to them for half an hour. Together, they laughed and sang several songs. After those praise songs, they reclined near a large table, talking, joking around, and enjoying what looked like appetizers. Their shadows were mimicking the movements they made that evening. They were all boisterous and laughing. Those disciples didn't seem like the men depicted in those religious movies or how they were described in Scripture. They seemed to be regular men whom Jesus hand-picked for the most crucial purpose and mission in their lives. Jesus sat at the center of the table, raised His hands toward heaven, and prayed. The room quickly became silent.

"I can't believe we're here to witness one of the most important historical events in Israel at the time. Wow, I am about to witness specific events before the Last Supper."

I whispered more to myself than to anyone.

"Yeah, Jesus is handsome, but not too handsome, average looking, come to think about it."

Karina whispered back to me.

"Corey, how's the restoration project going?"

"It's fine, Al. The full transfer will happen within 15 minutes."

"Great! Do you or Albert know how we can enter the time portal without changing this event or this time period? I mean, in fifteen minutes, we must extract ourselves from here. Wouldn't they ask us where we are going?"

"Wilma, as long as we don't show our devices and succinctly answer their question, we should be fine."

Karina leaned over to me.

"Dear, are you entirely sure about that?"

"Not 100%, but more certain of that than what caused Corey and I to travel towards the Gettysburg Address event and a time when a group of Confederate soldiers tried to assassinate Lincoln."

"There was an attempt on Lincoln's life before his assassination on April 15th, 1865?"

"Yes, I'll explain it all later on."

Karina nodded.

Jesus got up and took off His outer garment. He then tied a towel around His waist and poured water into a basin. He then went to one of His disciples and washed his feet. He did this to other disciples until He reached Peter, who said,

"Lord, are you going to wash my feet?"

Jesus replied,

"You do not realize now what I am doing, but later you will understand."

"No," said Peter, "you shall never wash my feet."

Jesus answered,

"Unless I wash you, you have no part with me."

"Then, Lord," Simon Peter replied, "not just my feet but my hands and my head as well."

He extended his hands after placing his feet in the basin. Jesus chuckled and answered,

"Those who have had a bath need only to wash their feet; their whole body is clean. And you are clean, though not every one of you."

"What made Jesus wash His disciples' feet?" Wilma said.

"He is showing that all His followers and disciples must serve others and each other. Love is serving others no matter who they are and what they do."

"Beep! Beep!"

The disciple looked around for the source of that odd sound. Some of them were frightened by the repeated sound. I quickly clicked my TVU to vibrate.

"Do you know what that signal means, Karina?" I spoke.

"No."

"Sweetie, it means that our Time Viewer Units are ready for our trip back home. We have thirty minutes to teleport out of here. Now we have the time to relax and witness one of the most important events in the Bible."

"Honey, are you sure it's okay for us to be here at all?"

"Yes dear, as long as we observe and do not participate in this event. No matter what happens here, observe. Do you understand?"

They all nodded.

"Al, are you there? Hello, anyone there?" Garcia radioed in.

The disciples and Jesus didn't hear her voice because my device's volume was low while loud enough for me to hear it. I grabbed my device from the satchel and hid it from Jesus and His disciples as I turned toward a wall.

"Yes Garcia, we are here."

I then walked to the far corner of that big room with my hand over my mouth and the device.

"Good, now what's your next step?"

"We will follow the entry sequence within 15 minutes."

"What? Why don't you guys leave right now?"

"We're going to witness the Last Supper live."

"Are you kidding me?"

Garcia shook her head in disbelief.

"You better leave within 15 minutes whether they finish their meal."

"I promise we will do that, Garcia."

I rejoined my group inconspicuously, not drawing any attention from those disciples or attendees, and put away my device into my satchel. We sat there observing every detail of the exchange between Jesus and His disciples.

Chapter 23

33 AD

After Jesus finished washing His disciples' feet, He put on His outer garment, returned to His place, and reclined at the table. He slowly raised his head to look at His disciples. His face showed great distress and concern.

"Wow! He really looks troubled about what will happen to Him in the next few hours."

"One of you will betray Me and hand Me over to the evildoers."

Everyone was confused by Jesus' statement. One of the disciples reclined towards Him and asked,

"Who is it, Lord?"

"It is the one to whom I will give this piece of bread when I have dipped it in the dish."

Jesus took a piece of bread, dipped it and hand it to Judas Iscariot. Judas ate it and then Jesus said to him,

"Do quickly what you are about to do."

Judas looked confusedly at Jesus, quickly got up, and then left without a word to anyone. The rest of the disciples were also confused. They wondered to each other on why Judas left the room. Jesus picked up a large bread and prayed over it. He took bread, and when He had given thanks, He broke it and gave it to His disciples, saying,

"Take it; this is my body."

Then He took a cup, and when He had given thanks, He gave it to them, and they all drank from it.

"This is My blood of the covenant, which is poured out for many," He said to them.

"Truly I tell you, I will not drink again from the fruit of the vine until that day when I drink it new in the kingdom of God."

Then they sang a hymn, which we didn't know. Yet, we still tried to follow with not much success.

"Beep!"

I quickly fetched my TVU, pressed a button on its screen, and whispered into it.

"Yes Garcia?"

I turned from the festive scene and brought my device to my face.

"On my end, your energy levels are at their maximum point. Are you now ready to leave?"

"We will leave in a couple of minutes. We must find a way to break away from Jesus and His disciples. We will signal you when you should start the countdown."

"Ok, Al. Your window to exit from your time period is narrowing every second. Garcia out!"

I flicked the switch to shut down my device's intercom and then looked at my three cohorts.

"Team, let's find a way to extricate ourselves from this proceeding and commence our journey home. We have seven minutes to do so."

I looked at my Apple watch and swiped its face for a different timer and energy recording for my mission.

"Guys, I hope this works."

"If my calculations are correct and my theory is sound, then I can enter a past time period or event as we travel through the portal to our present time period. I could also reenter the same portal to join my group without disrupting history."

This was one of many thoughts I conjured up as I looked at the energy readings from the time portal and within my TVU.

Jesus and His disciples rose from their place and exited the building. Our group did the same. Jesus looked at me as we stood in front of the building.

"Albert, lean on Me whenever you're lost or hurt for a long period of time. The devil wants to destroy you before you fulfill what God has planned for your life. I will continue to pray for wisdom, guidance, strength, and honesty to be given to you during your trial."

Jesus gathered his followers and headed to the Garden of Gethsemane while I led my group toward the Mount of Olives.

"Let's get to a clearing that will ensure that no one will detect our teleport back home."

We walked for a few minutes until we reached the desired spacing for our exit out of this time period. We were near the Mount of Olives. Trees were hiding the actual base of the mount, and this was where we stood, awaiting further instructions from Garcia.

I swiped my TVUs screen to look at my mathematical sequence, which opened up the time portal. I then pushed three buttons on the screen to reveal a second set of mathematical calculations to open a second portal. This second sequence will open thirty seconds after Karina and the rest of the group enter the first time portal. I will enter the second time portal at the thirty-second mark and travel to a different time period.

"I hope this works. I should be able to enter the second time portal, accomplish my mission, return to the first time portal, and intercept my group before reaching our present time period. In theory, they won't even notice my absence during their travel within the first time portal."

"Buzz!"

"Yes, Garcia?"

"Al, I noticed an anomaly regarding the time portal in your area. I don't think you should travel back to our time period until I know what we're dealing with now."

"What anomaly?"

I examined the readings on my device, and everything seemed fine. I quickly masked the increasing energy surge for my private trip with a few swipes on my TVU's screen.

"It seems any changes within the portal, slight or great, are detectable by our devices. I surely hope Garcia does not think much about it."

Garcia looked at her computer and TVU screens again and examined their readings. She found that all the readings had returned to normal, but she also found some other reading which was not supposed to be there. The strange energy flux and the appearance of another time portal opening were surprising to see at that moment. At first glance, many would not have noticed a thing, especially when you are not looking for any strange readings, yet with Garcia's trained eyes and a massive amount of time reading the different energy shifts whenever the portal opened, she was able to detect a slight change with the energy levels of the portal and TVU.

"Garcia, we are at the site for our entry into the present historical time period. We are fine and ready to return home."

"Great, Al. Now you need to initiate the teleporter from your site and send your destination code for the teleporter chamber to receive you guys."

"Got it," I turned to my three cohorts, "Now, let's prepare for our entry into the portal. We have 10 seconds upon entry. You three must stand closer as I punch in the

sequence."

Karina found that directive weird.

"Zap!"

All four beamed into the bright energy surge where the two portals opened simultaneously. Three of them entered one portal while I entered another portal.

"It worked! Now I'm off to fix the wrong I received many years ago."

I was satisfied with the new readings on my device and monitored the movements of my friends.

"Both missions are a go!"

Chapter 24

August 24, 2021– 2:25 PM

"That's strange? It seems some energy source has split away from the group. What is happening inside that portal?"

Garcia looked closer at those readings that suddenly appeared on her console screen. She punched in numbers, turned knobs, and moved levers to adjust the specs on her console. She then turned to the radar screen, tracking her four colleagues and the energy surges within the portal. Suddenly, she found a large package of energy separating from the primary energy pool within the four time traveler's huddle. Garcia shook her head, closed her eyes, and looked at the radar screen again. The energy was also surging within the Teleporter as the multiple lights flashed repeatedly and the alarms within the glass chamber sounded off. She turned a few knobs to bring those levels back to normal, but the readings continued to rise with each turn of the knob.

"What is causing that?"

Garcia clicked on a switch in an attempt to reach Karina or me, and then she remembered,

"We can't contact each other while they are traveling through the portal. Just great! We need to do something about that. I must note that in my calendar and personal notes for our next diagnostic meeting. We need open communication during movement through the portal in future missions."

"Hey Garcia, what's the status of the group?"

Robinson barged into the laboratory again. Garcia quickly clicks off the radar screen and console readings.

"They are on their way home, sir."

"Good. When will they reach the teleporter chamber? Can you give me their location?"

"I believe they will be here within 14 to 21 minutes, our time frame. As for their location, they are within the time portal en route to our time period."

Robinson looked at his watch.

"I will have a medical team here by that time. They will monitor them for any health issues due to their travels."

"Good sir. Now I need to return to my work if you don't mind?"

Garcia returned to her console and recorded the energy levels of the portal, the TVU, and the teleporter.

"Garcia, are you sure they will return without a hiccup from their established time period?"

"I can't make any promises."

"On that note, I will leave you be."

Robinson left the laboratory and then waved two agents over to him. He gave them orders, and they remained at the lab's entrance. He finally left the floor and then the building, as shown through our camera system throughout the building.

"I need to get some intel between Albert's team and Garcia. They have shut me out, but with my next visit, I will change that," Robinson thought as he entered his car.

Garcia was relieved that Robinson had left.

"Now I can focus on this energy shift from the main group."

She looked carefully at the radar and then at the console. She noticed the energy emitting from both circles on her radar was decreasing as if someone was sucking the energy from the portal through a straw.

"How am I going to tell them what will happen in the next seven minutes during their travel within the portal."

Garcia texted each team member, hoping one of our groups would receive it. The text alerted us about the energy anomaly and what may happen if we don't fix the developing problem quickly. Suddenly, Garcia froze in her tracks and remembered Corey's concerns for my well-being and the meaning of my new calculations. She flipped through Corey's binder to find any evidence that may tie the energy issue to my new calculations. None was found.

Chapter 25

No Time – within the time portal from August 24, 2021, and then exiting into May 3, 1974- 4:25 PM

After entering my time portal, I looked across the realm of tunnels and the flashing lights embedded into the literal webs of time and saw my wife with our friends traveling through their portal without a hitch. As the energy pulsed through their portal and mine, light shone through each portal into spaces, revealing other portals interconnecting within a space, unlike outer space. The area was dark except for the lights embedded in silky webs flashing between the portals and those shining throughout the portals. If I could move more than 30 miles from this area, the lights through the portal may look like twinkling stars. It was my first time seeing an area within and around time as empty airless cushions between portals. Then I suddenly realized that the portals were very fragile, thin tunnels that could shatter with slight pressure against them.

"I hope I have enough time and energy to accomplish my mission and the courage to end this time travel dream. Just traveling through these portals is dangerous enough to destroy time itself."

I looked at the readings on my TVU screen. I was also traveling to the future through a portal parallel to the one Karina, and the rest of our team were traveling through. Amazingly, they could not see me or notice my absence; I found that quite interesting.

"If I damage or destroy this time portal pathway, I will be unable to rendezvous with my Group, let alone get back to my past or present time period. So, I better get this right, or history, my own and everyone else's, will change forever."

I looked at my readings on the TVU screen and realized that my travel through this new portal would take longer than expected. What McGee did to the portal time variant has rippled through all time portals and possibly the entire time continuum. I must find a way to fix it before the ripple changes time forever, but I will do it after I finish both missions. I just realized that this ripple acts like an earthquake or aftershocks, which means there can be many shifts throughout the time continuum. As I slowly traveled through this portal, dreadful memories or different scenes of my life reared their ugly heads.

"The abuse I received from Coach Hood changed me as a young boy, which later manifested in my life as a man. My identity as a man was slightly cemented or imprinted by one particular role model, my father. He gave me a lot of rules and punishments due to my human errors. He was gone when I was twenty-two years old, and no male adult I could look up to or lean upon when I needed advice or proper bonding. I didn't receive trust, guidance, and comfort; on the flip side, I was given distrust, betrayal, and pain. Coach Hood was the first male figure to be interested in my life. After that abuse, I had difficulties relating with the opposite sex. I didn't feel comfortable, adequate, or worthy of developing meaningful relationships. Don't get me wrong, I was always attracted to females, but I felt uncomfortable and awkward around them. Through many of my short-lived dating relationships, I always tried to please my girlfriends for fear of losing their companionship. Through the years, I wondered why I behaved that way in every short- and long-term relationship. I continued to behave this way for many years, leading to meaningless relationships with no hope for marriage, a family, and a long-standing future. God revealed the reasons for my insecurities after accepting Jesus Christ as my personal Savior. By uncovering the abuse I endured, He answered my questions about why I failed with each relationship. After a while, I just wanted to be alone ever since the abuse. I often satisfied my

sexual desires alone, and afterward, I would yell at myself for succumbing to those desires. I just wanted for it, my sinful act, to stop!"

I found myself yelling within my mind as I wiped away my tears.

"This is ripping me apart. I must stop Coach Hood by any means to ensure a new timeline and create a secure and happy future."

"Zip!"

I tumbled into a busy hallway and crashed onto a wall full of pictures. My former middle school celebrates each month by putting up pictures of events or situations that occurred during a school day or after school. For example, the wall was entitled, "Monthly Events – May". Of course, several students laughed at my clumsy move. I smiled and looked at my Apple watch to set up my timer.

"I have ten minutes to complete my mission and get back with my team. My God, please help me while I try to do the right thing."

The boys and girls at that time period wore long hair and Levi's jeans. I quickly ducked into one of the janitorial closets. I put on the light and searched throughout the entire small closet. I found a janitor's uniform but decided to change into the teacher's clothes of that time period, which I had in my satchel.

"I would benefit from easier access and movement through the school as a teacher or substitute."

I left the closet and blended with the moving crowd in search of my younger self or Coach Hood, preferably the latter.

"Beep! Beep!"

I quickly took out my device and silenced it. I then opened the text message on its screen.

"Al, what are you doing? You forgot that I could track your movements through the time portal. This is a feature you installed just in case you get trapped within the time portal or another time period."

"Great! Now Garcia knows generally where and when I exited the teleporter, but I am not sure she knows the exact date I have entered since the time tracker can only give a range of time, a decade or two. What will she do with this bit of information?"

I had to return a reply, or she may tell Karina what I was doing.

"Garcia, I need to do this. The event I'm about to erase has haunted me all my life. I can't bear it anymore. I hope my plan to eliminate the cause of my pain will work. The person who caused this suffering will only affect my immediate timeline, and that is the same person I need to erase."

"Al, you're about to kill someone! Please don't do it! I believe and know in my heart that's not you."

"Don't worry, Garcia. I'm just fine. Just don't tell Karina."

There was no reply. I put my device into the satchel as I bumped into a middle-aged man.

"Oh, excuse me."

"No problem, man. We all have to get where we're going. You have a good day, my boy."

I cringed at the familiar sound of those words and stopped in my tracks. I quickly looked back at the man.

"That was Coach Hood!"

Lord Jesus, I Need You

by Simple Truth

Oh Lord, my heart is aching.
I feel so lost right now.
I woke up th s morning.
And I looked everywhere for You.
Yet You are with me
And I don't need to look far.
Lord Jesus, I need You today
Lord Jesus, I need You tonight
Lord Jesus, I need You every day
Oh Lord Jesus, I just need You
I praise You Lord, for all You have done for me
I praise You Lord, for Your promises
My Lord, I thank You
My Lord, I thank You
I thank You for everything
Lord Jesus, I need You today
Lord Jesus, I need You tonight
Lord Jesus, I need You every day

Oh Lord Jesus, I just need You
My Lord Jesus, You have never let me go
Since I surrendered to You and repented
Even when I sin because I am still a sinner
You have never left me
Yet I fear Your righteous wrath
I believe in You and what You did for me
So I cry out
Lord Jesus, I need You today
Lord Jesus, I need You tonight
Lord Jesus, I need You every day
Oh Lord Jesus, I just need You

Chapter 26

May 3, 1974 – 4:35 PM

The bathroom was not well-lit, and a slither of light came through the breaks between the uneven wallpaper covering the bathroom windows. Those darkened windows prevented any peeping toms from looking in, while it gave the room an ominous look and frightening feel, like a dark, cold cave or castle room from Medieval times.

Any young child would feel trapped by the heavy darkness surrounding them with no hope of escaping. That's why many boys entered the bathroom in pairs or small groups. Yet few would enter without that wisdom. Abruptly, there was heavy breathing from one of the bathroom stalls and whispers of a young boy with an overwhelming raspy breathing sound. The young boy was me.

"No!" the small voice yelped through the darkness.

"Don't worry; you will like it," a dark, heavy voice said.

The boy was me. I banged against the stall door and wall with no one to help me. The combination of old cologne and oily, dirty sweat reeked through the bathroom. I turned towards the odor and saw a curtain of yellow-stained teeth as Coach Hood smiled.

"There is no one here to help you. I sent everyone home since I have you to help me collect the gym equipment. Aren't we friends, Albert?"

"No! We are not friends! Help! Someone help me! Please God, help me!"

My cries echoed from the stall and through the bathroom. There was no one there to answer my cries. Coach Hood grabbed me and molested me to the point of fully satisfying his lustful desires. After what seemed to be an eternity of abuse within that short time span, Coach Hood released me.

"*You can go home now. I'll clean up here. Remember, nothing happened here, Albert. If I hear anything about this, you will be off the team, and I will make your life a living hell. Now, you have a good day, my boy.*"

The memory of that afternoon continued to haunt me every day since being born again and becoming a Christian, even when I returned to the very time period I wanted to change. I raised my head to look at a sign across a large door frame that stated:

'Boys Locker Room.'

Before I walked through that door frame, I looked at the hallway clock, which showed – 4:35 PM.

"*It will happen in seven minutes.*"

I tried to shake off those memories as tears slowly flowed down my cheeks.

"*This moment still feels fresh as if it happened yesterday. The pain is real, yet the details of the abuse have changed. I know he harmed my body, heart, and soul.*"

The children scurrying to and from the locker room were athletes who had just finished their respective workouts. Coach Hood was heading to the locker room while I was a few feet behind him. Once I entered the locker room, I heard him and my younger counterpart talking.

"Come on, Albert. I need to show you something," Coach Hood said.

"I don't need to go there. You can show me whatever you want to out here."

"No, it's a secret, and I just want it to be between us."

"A secret? Really? And you want to tell me? What is it?"

I entered the bathroom, going after my younger counterpart and Coach Hood as they entered one of the stalls. I carefully went to the sink and started to wash my hands. I looked at myself in that familiar, cracked mirror.

"I have to do this so I can be totally free from him," I whispered, trying to convince myself.

I dried my hands and pulled a .45 caliber handgun from my jacket pocket.

"No Al! Put it away. Put your trust in Me. Killing Coach Hood will not erase the hurt, your anguish, and emptiness," a peaceful voice called out, which I heard audibly.

"I want to release myself from this pain, Lord. I want to be free."

Tears were starting to trickle down my cheeks.

"Then give Me your burdens and lean on Me. I will give you everlasting comfort and peace from this painful memory," my Lord God said to me.

My hands were shaking as I took several steps toward the occupied stall. I heard my younger counterpart bang against the bathroom stall door. I reached for the bathroom stall door but froze with fear and uncertainty. I could not take another step while I didn't steady the gun.

"Lord, how can I leave him without protection against this evil?"

"Al, I was there when it happened, and I cried out into Coach Hood's mind, but he didn't listen."

"Lord, You have the power to stop it, but You just let it happen. Why?"

"Al, I am not to enter history abruptly and disturb it. I can only enter with a gentleman's agreement by influencing and speaking into people's lives. They must decide which way to go and follow throughout their lives."

"You're God! You can stop him with a snap of Your fingers!"

"Albert, I gave free will to you, Coach Hood, and all of mankind. My creation has the freedom to decide which way it will go. Now put away your gun, return to your wife, and preserve this timeline."

"Listen to Him. He would never leave you or forsake you."

A shadowy figure came from my left side and then moved to my right side.

"Trust Him."

The shadowy figure quickly moved from the bathroom stall to the entrance and back to the locker room. I tried to keep up with the figure's motions with my eyes but lost sight of its presence. A sudden burst of light came into the locker room and throughout the bathroom. The shadowy figure seemed to enter that light and then disappeared as that light faded.

"I must have spoken to the Holy Spirit."

I stood there for a couple of minutes and finally relented from my plan. I retreated to another bathroom stall and listened to what unfolded behind the stall's wall. I yelped internally and shook violently to the core of my heart. Through a slit along the stall door, I witnessed my young counterpart exiting from the cell-like stall next to me while fixing his pants and trying to smooth out his shirt with his tiny hands. He went to the nearest sink to clean his hands and face. My young counterpart raised his head and looked at himself in the mirror with great shame. He fixed his hair and then shook with disgust as well as fear, which caused him to take a couple of steps from the sink. He then crumbled next to the sink and cried out with loud sobs, but no one was there to hear him.

"God help me! Please help me!"

My young counterpart got up and ran out of the bathroom, through the locker room, and into the hallway. I also left the locker room to see where I went but was unsuccessful.

"I will never look back on this day as I did during my youth. I buried it since God did not do a thing for me."

I went through the long hallways to find the nearest exit. As I walked out of the school, I pressed a sequence of codes on my Time Viewer Unit and sent myself back to my wife and team.

"Lord, how can I get rid of this pain and anguish other than saying, 'I released it to you, my Lord.'?"

"Only through forgiveness can you find peace and healing from this terrible anguish and wrong in your life, Albert. So, you need to forgive Coach Hood."

"What?"

"Zap!"

"You heard Me!"

How Can I Forgive?

by Promised Gifts

Lord, You forgave me years ago.
   When I was a dreadful sinner and was worthless
   Yet You surrendered Your throne, Your Body
   And released Your Blood in place of the wrath I deserve
   How can You forgive me?
   After all the things I did against You
   How can You forgive me?
   When I don't ever deserve Your love
   How can You forgive me?
   How can You forgive me?
   Others violated me
   My heart grew angry toward them
   Yet You spoke to my heart
   'Forgive them, My child, as I forgave you.'
   How can I forgive them?
   After they violated my body, heart, and soul
   How can I forgive them?
   After those memories torture me throughout my life

How can I forgive them?
How can I forgive them?
Forgive them, my child, as I forgave the Roman soldiers
Forgive them, my child, as I forgave the Jewish leaders
Forgive them, my child, as I forgave the criminal on the cross
Forgive them, my child, as I forgave you

Chapter 27

July 2, 1863 – 4 PM to 7 PM

I opened my eyes.

"Forgive him? How can I forgive that person? Who would even want to…?"

Before I could finish my thought of that ridiculous request from God, I noticed a disturbing thing as I traveled through the portal. The scenes along the portal walls moved faster than usual, making interpreting difficult. The speed didn't help my body since I was getting sick with each passing moment, hurling through the portal. As I continued traveling at a high velocity, I lost all sense of time and all of my senses in my body.

"Am I heading to the past, the future, or forever stuck in this perpetual loop traveling an endless portal? I don't know what's going on with this portal. I felt like I was traveling through a big Tilt-a-whirl at tremendously high speed while heading nowhere fast. God help me!" I thought and prayed.

As quickly as I entered the portal, I was ejected onto a hill with thick trees in all directions. I rolled down the hill as I yelled.

"Help! Help! Help me!"

There was no answer as I continued to roll until I hit a tree against my upper torso. Luckily, I didn't break anything. I just got the wind knocked out of me. As I took a few minutes to regain my breath, I got up to survey the area and tried to grasp what time period I had entered.

"Bang! Bang!"

"Boom!"

My body shook with each explosion and small pop.

"I'm in a war zone! Which war? What country? What year?"

I tried to run away as quickly as possible from those loud sounds. Unfortunately, I could not outrun them because of the repetitive gunfire and explosions around me.

"Great! I entered the middle of a war zone and can't find a way out of it."

I looked for cover and found a large tree with a few bushes next to it. I quickly took out my TVU and smacked it several times to find out where and when I was. The device pinged and showed.

"Gettysburg, PA, USA, July 2, 1863 – 4 PM"

I shook my head in disbelief.

"How did this happen?"

I didn't send a message to Garcia informing her of my sudden diversion to this time period. I couldn't send a message dealing with my demons to anyone because I was not supposed to travel through time alone, even for my own personal vendetta.

"Bang! Bang!"

The gunfire was coming closer. I ran from the tree to a huge boulder and waited there until the gunfire decreased or hopefully stopped. Instead, the intensity and volume of those gun fires increased and were advancing towards me. Within minutes, the battle continued near and around me. I was surrounded and had nowhere to hide, so I secretly joined the nearest infantry.

"I need to get out of here, or I will be a casualty of this Civil War."

I rubbed my TVU like a Genie bottle, trying to stir it back to life in my desperate attempt to reenter the portal. Unfortunately, I was unsuccessful, and my only temporary refuge was a Union infantry group within a line of other infantries along the top of a small hill.

"Colonel Chamberlain, you are at the extreme left of the Union Army. You are not to retreat or surrender. You must hold on unto the last men, rifle, or bullet."

A commanding officer gave him this order as General Lee planned a sweeping attack on the high ground. I looked around to find all the soldiers belonging to that infantry double-lined there, ready for a surge from the Confederates.

"This was the battle of Little Round Top."

I watched the men get ready by loading their rifles and aiming toward the lower part of the hill. They were anticipating a charge from the Confederates.

"How will I get out of here without help from Garcia, Corey, or Kari? I can only hope I am able to very soon."

"Here they come!" yelled an officer.

I moved behind an officer, whom I later learned was Colonel Lawrence Chamberlain, to stay out of the line of fire during their charge. His infantry fired continuously through the Confederate's assault. During the Confederate's offensive surges, officers quickly gave their report and line status to Chamberlain. The first officer was Buster. He was a short, pudgy man with an Irish accent, while the other was Tom Chamberlain, Colonel Chamberlain's brother, with a thick mustache and sideburns.

The constant firing from the Union line and the Confederate counterparts produced a smoky film throughout the thickets of trees that lined the hill. I coughed and gagged a few times since I was not used to it at all. Throughout the battlefield, hundreds of dead men lay along the ground between the trees, leaning on many of them and boulders. There were just over fifty in one small section and hundreds in others. The bloody odor nearly knocked me out, and I felt steadily nauseous during this battle scene. A soldier bumped into me just when I was about to pass out and brought me back to reality, as all eyes were trained on the inevitable upcoming second surge from the Confederates. I took out my Time Viewer Unit, put it on, and looked for any chance to enter the time portal and get back to my team. Incredibly, the device had some difficulty reading the time portal and bringing up enough power to open it. I shook my head as I felt a wave of stress run through my whole body. I put away my device, knelt, and prayed.

"Lord Jesus, help me get back with my team. Yes, I have ill feelings towards Coach Hood, and I still want You to kill him, but I need Your help to overcome this hatred. I ask this through Jesus Christ, Amen."

Tom Chamberlain pats me on my shoulder.

"Please pray for the men and me as well."

"I will, sir."

He continued walking through the line, encouraging his men. The third surge died down for a few minutes until another wave started up the hill. During that fourth wave of Confederates charging up the hill, a shot rang out and hit Colonel Chamberlain, knocking him backward. Several men raced to him and helped him up.

"Thank you, men."

Chamberlain looked at his sword and saw a large indentation.

"Wow! Incredible. Praise God!"

After he shook off that shock, he continued to give orders to his unit and command them with more vigor than before as the Confederate's fourth wave came up the small hill. With each wave, I heard the constant clattering of the men's equipment upon their bodies as they marched or ran up the hill. Of course, there was constant rifle fire throughout each charge, but there were momentary pockets of silence.

"Colonel!"

"Yes?"

"Many of our men are either low or out of ammunition."

"Colonel, many of our men throughout the line have no ammunition. What can we do?" another soldier reported.

"Make every shot count and recover any ammunition from your dead or wounded comrades."

A fifth wave came upon them, and the infantry held them off again.

"Colonel, we don't have enough ammunition to withstand another charge," Tom reported.

"How about any supplies from other companies?"

"They don't have any to spare," another soldier reported.

The colonel lowered his head and then slowly raised it.

"Ok, we will f x bayonets."

"What?" Tom said.

"Order everyone to fix bayonets. We are going to charge down the hill. Those reb boys are tired and weary. We have the advantage of charging downhill. Send the order to fix bayonets."

The officers begrudgingly moved to their divisions, ordering, "Fix bayonets!"

Chamberlain also emphatically gave the same order to anyone who could hear it. Then suddenly, another wave of Confederates came forward with rifles and guns blazing. Chamberlain yelled, "Charge!"

Then, the left flank quickly ran forward with their bayonets pointed toward the Confederates. My TVU kicked in with full power as I ran with the troops. I pressed three buttons and instantly entered the portal, moving towards my team.

"Zap!"

"Thank you, my Lord God! Thank you!"

Chapter 28

585 BC

After a quick journey through the time portal, I was hurled into a crowd moving towards a large tower; at least, it looked similar to the Freedom Tower in shape and height from where I was sitting. The people hugged and cradled each other, trying to squelch their fears as many soldiers gathered together. I got up and brushed off any dust from my 1863 outfit. Conspicuously, I took out my Time Viewer Unit to get a handle on what type of predicament I was in at that time period. I also wanted to know the historical significance of the event I entered and what I needed to do to prevent any changes in those historical facts. I put it on, and it gave me a quick read of the area and time period. It gave me the following:

585 BC – Shadrach, Meshach, Abednego, and the Fiery Furnace.

I did a double-take with my TVU screen and then closed it.

"If I don't return to my original portal with my friends, I will be stuck here forever. How am I going to get out of here?"

I joined the crowd, walking for at least 30 minutes to an hour towards a large wall surrounding a great city. The crowd stopped moving, and I witnessed everyone staring over the wall. I looked at what everyone was staring at and suddenly stopped in my tracks. I was looking at the most humongous statue I had ever witnessed. It was made of gold with its facial image similar to a man I saw sitting on his throne.

"Who is that man? Is he a king or just a provincial ruler? Oh, hold on! Now I remember this Bible story. Where are those three men who were listed on my TVU screen?"

I heard this name repeatedly mentioned in the crowd: Nebuchadnezzar. He must be their king. He ordered the people to bow or fall down as the horn, flute, lyre, trigon, psaltery, and bagpipe played. I got closer to the king and his men to understand what was happening. Everyone fell down to worship the statue, except three men. Well, I didn't worship the statue, either. I hid myself from the king and his men.

I heard Nebuchadnezzar's advisers telling him:

"O king, live forever! You, O king, have made a decree that every person who hears the sound of the horn, flute, lyre, trigon, psaltery, and bagpipe, and all kinds of musical instruments, is to fall down and worship the golden statue. But whoever does not fall down and worship shall be thrown into the middle of a furnace of blazing fire. There are certain Jews whom you have appointed over the administration of the province of Babylon, namely Shadrach, Meshach, and Abed-nego. These men, O king, have disregarded you; they do not serve your gods, nor do they worship the golden statue which you have set up."

Then Nebuchadnezzar in rage and anger gave orders to bring Shadrach, Meshach, and Abed-nego; then these men were brought before the king. I tried my TVU to find a way to leave that time period.

"I need to get back with my team, or there may be repercussions with the time continuum."

"Beep!"

I quickly silenced my device and looked at its screen.

"No portal access at this time!"

I shook the device, hoping to erase that message like I used to with my Etch-a-Sketch toy. Of course, the message stared right back at me. I put the TVU back into my satchel when the three men whom the king summoned stood in front of the throne. Nebuchadnezzar began speaking and said to them,

"Is it true, Shadrach, Meshach, and Abed-nego, that you do not serve my gods, nor worship the golden statue that I have set up? Now if you are ready, at the moment you hear the sound of the horn, flute, lyre, trigon, psaltery, and bagpipe, and all kinds of musical instruments, to fall and worship the statue that I have made, very well. But if you do not worship, you will immediately be thrown into the midst of a furnace of blazing fire; and what god is there who can rescue you from my hands?"

Shadrach, Meshach, and Abed-nego replied to the king,

"Nebuchadnezzar, we are not in need of an answer to give you concerning this matter. If it be so, our God whom we serve is able to rescue us from the furnace of blazing fire; and He will rescue us from your hand, O king. But even if He does not, let it be known to you, O king, that we are not going to serve your gods nor worship the golden statue that you have set up."

Then Nebuchadnezzar was filled with wrath, and his facial expression was changed toward Shadrach, Meshach, and Abed-nego. He answered by giving orders to heat the furnace seven times more than it was usually heated. And he ordered certain valiant warriors who were in his army to tie up Shadrach, Meshach, and Abed-nego in order to throw them into the furnace of blazing fire. Then these men were tied up in their trousers, their coats, their caps, and their other clothes, and were thrown into the middle of the furnace of blazing fire. For this reason, because the king's command was harsh and the furnace had been made extremely hot, the flame of the fire killed those men who took up Shadrach, Meshach, and Abed-nego. But these three men, Shadrach, Meshach, and Abed-nego, fell into the middle of the furnace of blazing fire still tied up.

"Buzz! Buzz!"

I took out my vibrating device and looked at its screen. It stated,

"Portal access available within 12 minutes."

I smiled with relief as I returned my TVU to my satchel. I looked at the furnace and prayed for those three men. Then Nebuchadnezzar the king was astounded and stood up quickly; he said to his counselors,

"Was it not three men that we threw bound into the middle of the fire?"

They replied to the king,

"Absolutely, O king."

He responded,

"Look! I see four men untied and walking about in the middle of the fire unharmed, and the appearance of the fourth is like a son of the gods!"

Then Nebuchadnezzar came near to the door of the furnace of blazing fire; he said,

"Shadrach, Meshach, and Abed-nego, come out, you servants of the Most High God, and come here!"

Then Shadrach, Meshach, and Abed-nego came out of the middle of the fire. The satraps, the prefects, the governors, and the king's counselors gathered together and saw that the fire had no effect on the bodies of these men, nor was the hair of their heads singed, nor were their trousers damaged, nor had even the smell of fire touched them.

Nebuchadnezzar responded and said,

"Blessed be the God of Shadrach, Meshach, and Abed-nego, who has sent His angel and rescued His servants who put their trust in Him, violating the king's command, and surrendered their bodies rather than serve or worship any god except their own God. Therefore, I make a decree that any people, nation, or population of any language that speaks anything offensive against the God of Shadrach, Meshach, and Abed-nego shall be torn limb from limb and their houses made a rubbish heap, because there is no other god who is able to save in this way."

Then the king made Shadrach, Meshach, and Abed-nego prosperous in the province of Babylon. My heart was full of joy for those men, but I had some reservations.

"Lord, you entered into time for those three men. Why can't you enter my life and fix it?"

There was no answer. My TVU vibrated again, and I quickly looked at its screen.

"Three minutes to Portal Entry!"

I walked away from that miraculous scene to a clearing behind the golden statue. I pressed the green button on my TVU and instantly entered the portal.

"Zip!"

My Rescue

by Sanctification Group

Lord, for most of my life, I felt alone
   The circumstances of loss and grieve
   Followed me everywhere I traveled
   The emptiness grew heavier with every step I took
   Yet Lord, You are my Rescue
   I look to You as Thomas did in the upper room
   And I have no choice but to say, 'My Lord and My God!'
   I crashed my car, and you rescued me
   I choked on a sandwich, and you rescued me
   I was drowning, and you rescued me
   I had a golf ball sized tumor in my chest, and you rescued me
   My shoulders were torn up with much pain, and you rescued me
   A past abuse tormented me, and you rescued me
   You are my Rescue
   You took me from the depths of depression
   You are my Rescue
   You blessed me with healing through your stripes
   You are my Rescue
   You renewed my life through your blood
   You are my Rescue, Father God

You are my Rescue, Holy Spirit
Hallelujah!
You are my Rescue, Jesus, the Son of God

Chapter 29

No Time – Within the Time Portal (Originally sent out through it on August 24, 2021)

Within the time portal, flashes of colorful light were moving in all directions and flowing around my team. Karina looked behind her, then towards her left side, and finally to her right side, trying to find me, but I wasn't there.

"Now, where is he? He was just behind us when we entered the portal."

I was still within my portal from 1974, moving quickly towards the homeward-bound portal my team was traveling through. I saw them through the respective walls of each portal we traveled through. As I looked at them, two distant memories came to mind.

~

It was a cold day on January 21, 1981, at 5:00 PM. While sitting at my desk, I read several studies dealing with Crohn's disease, stomach cancer, and their causality within our bodies. This was my research work during my junior year in college because my dad had those diseases. I wrote a paper during my sophomore year, and then afterward, I delved deeper into the vast work of those diseases. This memory brought me to that very year, towards the end of his remission, dealing with those dreadful diseases.

"Knock! Knock!"

I pulled back my head in aggravation. I quickly closed my research books and opened my textbook and notebook for my biology class.

"Yes, Dad, come in."

The door opened slowly.

"Was I that obvious? I've been a frequent visitor, huh?"

He had visited my room during my studies for at least three days every week.

"Nah, Dad! It's ok. I enjoy your company."

I bit my lip with that lie.

"I actually needed time to study for tomorrow's important Biology exam," I thought.

I shared my room with my brother for the past 18 years, but at that time, he was attending Georgetown University in DC. We had two full-sized beds on either side of the room. Dad walked gingerly to the end of my bed and sat on it. I didn't immediately look at him. I just stared at the same words on a particular page of my biology textbook.

"I know I have been bothering you, but I have a lot to give to you before...."

Dad's voice trailed off. I turned to him.

"Dad, you're in remission right now. I believe you can beat this disease."

"I also believe that son, but I haven't been a good father lately."

"What do you mean?"

"Fathers are supposed to prepare their sons for the world. Teach them how to be a father and raise a family."

"Dad, I have learned a lot from what I witnessed on how you ran this family throughout my whole life."

"True, but advice from me can go a long way. Al, I know you follow the beat of your own drum, but there might be some things I can offer to help you navigate through difficult situations down your life road."

I looked at my books and then at my dad's aging face. He looked between 68 and 78 years old, while he was really 55 years old. I closed my physics book and turned towards him.

"Ok Dad, I'm all ears."

"With all of the things I have imparted to you, there is one thing I hope and pray will resonate within your heart and soul."

I raised my eyebrows.

"What's that?"

"As you know, all actions have consequences, good or bad, but most importantly, you cannot go back to those past actions and change them. Those events, for what they are worth, make you into who you are and what you will become. Do you understand?"

"Yeah, Dad, I got it. I am the product of what I do, how I respond to people by how they treat me, and how I go out of my way to treat people properly."

Dad lovingly tapped my leg.

"Yes, that's it!"

I quickly moved my leg from him, which he didn't notice. Instead, he got up and started for the bedroom door.

"Son, I wish I could witness your successes and how you will become a fine man."

I didn't say a word and stared at his slow exit from my room.

The second memory was clearer and more precise:

It was a sunny day on May 3, 1983, at 6:30 PM.

"Negra! Ayudame!"

A middle-aged, dark-skinned woman enters the bathroom to find her husband on the toilet seat done with moving his bowels. She quickly closed the door once she got inside.

"Stuck again, Honey?"

"Yeah, I don't have the strength to push off this toilet seat."

It was evident that he had no strength to stand up from a toilet seat since the chemo he took so he could battle his cancer ravished his body. I was twenty-two years old with little knowledge of how the body reacts to chemotherapy, let alone to the devastating effects of cancer growth through-out his body.

"My strength is not enough to pull you off the seat. I need some help."

"No dear. He won't be able to help you. Instead, he will make a mess over here."

I was at the door listening to my parent's discourse and lowered my head, saddened by my dad's words. It was amazing how a man decimated by chemotherapy for the past three years could still stab me with his words. I started to walk away when suddenly the bathroom door swung open.

"Al, can you help me with your dad?"

I slowly turned around to find my Dad seated on the toilet seat while my mom stood beside him.

"Sure, Mom."

I walked to the other side of him, and on the count of three, Mom and I were able to lift him from the toilet seat. Since he was stuck for more than ten minutes, his legs were numb, and he needed a few minutes to wake them up. Dad shuffled his feet for a few feet until I reached over to hold his arm and balanced him. He immediately pulled away from my grasp and continued to move with a considerable lack of balance. With every step, he braced himself by laying his hands and forearms upon the hallway walls. I was hurt by his shrugging me away when I offered my assistance, but I remained behind him, ready to catch him if he fell. Once he reached the living room, he made a slow beeline for his recliner. Once he reached it, he turned around and sat down at a semi-slow speed. He pulled the side handle bringing his chair into a horizontal position. Almost immediately, his eyes rolled back, and his breathing became very mechanical, slowing down with each minute. Within three minutes, my dad died. I looked at him, wondering where he had gone. A tear flowed slowly down my right cheek until I wiped it off. My dad was dead at 57 years old.

"How can I move forward? I wish I could reconfigure time and prevent my dad's death. I didn't even have a chance to tell him, 'I love you and thank you.'"

I just stood there watching my mom caressing my dad's bald head and saying,

"I love you, Honey. Now, you are no longer in pain. Rest mi amor."

His body was very still and turning pale with each second.

"Man, his doctor lied to him and the entire family. My Dad was never going to look like his young, muscular self. There has to be a way to change the result of his suffering from those diseases and treatments from ending with his death. I promise you, Dad, that I will return to this time period and save you."

~

I shook my head from that distant memory and wiped my tears away. I rubbed my face, realizing that certain memories haunt you for years, as this one did for me. After accepting Jesus Christ fifteen years after my father's death, I didn't entertain the notion of changing my personal history.

"I wonder what you think of me, Dad, with this dilemma dealing with Coach Hood, who you thought was a great guy."

Suddenly a brief, bright flash appeared behind the trio as if something forced itself into their portal. I felt a force pull me out of the 1974 portal and push me into the homeward-bound portal, which moved me quickly to my wife.

"Hey Sweetie, missed me?"

Karina jumped a bit and then turned towards me.

"Yeah, I thought we left you behind with Jesus and His disciples."

"No, I was just running behind within the portal after I took care of something."

"Really? What was that something?"

"I can't say right now."

"Corey and Wilma are far behind us. They won't hear us, and we can whisper, babe. Wouldn't that make you feel more comfortable talking about that?"

Karina grabbed my hand to encourage me to spill my guts as I looked around to confirm her statement.

"Okay, here it goes. I was not in the portal with you guys. I had to go back to 1974 to take care of something. I am so sorry for lying. Please forgive me."

"Honey, I forgive you. It must be a great 'something' you needed to take care of and to risk the entire mission. You could have destroyed the time continuum or damaged our timeline irreparably. What was the 'something' you needed to take care of?"

"When I tried to get back to you, the time portal hurdled me to Gettysburg circa 1863. It took me a moment to enter this time portal, and I was determined to get here."

I gave a nervous smile as I ignored her question.

"Al, please give me your reason for risking your existence in our time period and possibly risking our return home."

Karina squeezed my hand as I looked at her beautiful face. She grinned and gave me an encouraging nod. I relented and explained the entire abusive episode I received at twelve years old, the angry flashes throughout my life since then, and my present distractions while building the Teleporter and with this present mission. Karina listened intently and asked questions periodically. She even rubbed my hand when it was difficult for me to speak about that tragic incident and the pain in my heart and soul. Once everything was off my chest, she hugged me.

"I love you more now than ever before. God willing, I will always be by your side, Al."

"Now our Lord God wants me to forgive Coach Hood and preach the Good News to him. Isn't that weird?"

"No, it's profound and biblical."

"What?"

"Al, remember what Jesus said. We're to love one another to be considered His, and we are to love our enemies."

"Kari, it's too hard to do that. How can I forgive and love him after what he did to me?"

"Yes, that's a tough one. Truthfully, I would have difficulty forgiving a person who molested me."

"You see, even you admit you can't do it. I am not Jesus, so how can I forgive my abuser?"

"Al, remember when Jesus was nailed to the cross, and He forgave the Roman soldiers for their part in His death? He did it as he was dying on the cross. Now that's really loving your enemies."

I remained silent as we traveled through the portal. I looked forward as the kaleidoscope colors within the portal continued to flow around the group.

"How does one release their hatred and anger towards a person who has hurt you, and then miraculously turn around to love that same person?"

I closed my eyes, and tears streamed down my cheeks.

"The various actions you committed against Me are sin. You had hurt and grieved Me. When you accepted Me and repented from those actions, through My blood, I forgave and cleansed you from all iniquities and gave you the

Holy Spirit. I love you, Al, and this was shown when I took the cross to take upon the wrath you deserved. Now, you are on the way to Heaven, and Coach Hood deserves the same chance you received. I did this wonderful work for all of mankind. He can also receive my grace if he believes in Me, ask for forgiveness, and repent his sins."

I nodded as the tears continued to flow down my cheeks. Karina didn't notice, and I was glad she didn't. I quickly dried my face and looked away from her. We continued through the portal without a hitch.

Lord, I Need You

by Redemption Group

Lord, I need You
   Without You, I am lost
   Thank You for Your Word
   Lord, I need You
   Lord, I love You
   Your love is unconditional
   How can I love others in that way?
   Who am I that You value so much to rescue?
   This is why my Lord, I love You
   Lord, I hear You
   Thank You for speaking to me
   I cherish Your Voice and what You have said to me
   Please give me the words to speak to others
   Lord, I hear You
   Hallelujah to You, my Lord Jesus
   I can't wait for Your coming
   Oh Lord, I am waiting for You
   Because my Lord Jesus, I need You

Chapter 30

August 24, 2021– 2:45 PM

Robinson returned to the lab and found Garcia staring intently at her computer screen, unaware of his entrance.

"I can tell her I got nothing from McGee later on."

He slowly approached his former agent.

"Garcia, what's the status of our team?"

Garcia jumped a bit and then turned towards Robinson.

"Really? How often does he need to startle me to ensure I know he can sneak up on me anytime?"

She returned her attention to the console screen and observed different readings from the three TVUs synchronized with her device within the portal. Garcia was also disturbed by what she found.

"They should have arrived by now, but it seems they were delayed by something, and I am not sure what's causing it."

Garcia lied as she looked at Robinson and then returned her gaze to the console and radar screens.

"I sure hope they're coming soon. Your calculations with each teleport trip have been off in minutes, not seconds."

Robinson leaned over the teleport console and slowly moved his right hand underneath it to check his tiny triangular device.

"It seems secure. I need to see if it's still functioning."

He pulled his car keys from his pants pocket and purposely dropped them under the console.

"Oh great!"

Robinson bent down to retrieve his keys. He slowly grabbed them and looked at his recording device.

"The green light indicates that the machine is working just fine."

Suddenly, the glass chamber revved up to receive the four-time travelers. Garcia jerked her head up while Robinson jumped up to his feet.

"Finally, they are coming back home."

"I can see that, but you admit you have some reservations about the teleporter. There have been too many delays with each teleport."

"The team has discussed it, and we have a couple of theories for the teleport delays, but I am not ready to share them now."

The chamber increased its revving, which absorbed more energy from the portal.

"In seven seconds, they will be here."

Garcia turned back to the chamber and looked at her console while she rotated a couple of knobs and flipped a switch.

"Zip!"

Karina, Corey, Wilma, and I appeared in the chamber in a sudden flash. Karina and I leaned upon each other for support while Corey sat down as Wilma slouched against the chamber's glass wall. Overall, we were alive and well enough to exit the chamber in our own power slowly. Robinson quickly grabbed each of our hands and shook them,

"Great job! You're heroes in the 10th order. You and your cohorts will receive the Presidential Medal of Honor for your great work in this mission."

I held on to Robinson's hand and locked eyes with him.

"No, Eugene, we will not receive any medal of honor publicly or privately. This was a secret mission the public will never get wind of, and rightfully so."

Robinson released my hand.

"Well, maybe we can honor you in private. In the meantime, we can use your teleporter to help mankind."

"Agent Robinson, the teleporter is not for sale, and I will not release it to the government."

I left the lab with my arm wrapped around Karina's shoulder.

"Well, stop by my office so I can give you a report on McGee."

I left the lab without another word. Corey and Wilma also left without any fanfare. Robinson wondered as he left the lab a few minutes after them,

"Will there be any more missions for this teleporter and with those scientists?"

Garcia was about to shut down the chamber when she caught sight of an energy spray from another portal. She magnified it on her computer and console screens, then lay a trace from the point of her sighting to its origin.

"What? Why is it coming from that time period? How is that possible when this time portal they traveled through came from ancient Jerusalem? Is this related to Albert's illicit trip?"

Garcia continued her investigation, which went into the wee hours of the evening. Unbeknownst to her, she discovered more than she bargained for.

Chapter 31

After our 1865 rescue mission, I rested and journaled my insights on my relationship with Jesus Christ and wrote notes on the different theories dealing with the time portal delays, the various hiccups within the portal, and improvements for the Teleporter. One great development that occurred during our hiatus from my lab work and Karina's teaching assignments was the fact that she gained weight due to a lively baby within her womb.

On this day, Karina and I decided to return to my NYU laboratory, not to reminisce on our first mission. Instead, we gathered more of my technical notes and statistical data dealing with our previous mission and the various time portal readings.

"Hey, Al! Hey Karina! What brings you here?"

Garcia covered her investigative work on my unauthorized trip and other aspects of the Teleporter, i.e., our inability to contact a team while traveling through a time portal, inexplicable rumbles through the portal, and our inadvertent entrance to different time periods.

"It's ok, Garcia. Karina found out I was feeding you intel dealing with the upgrades to the Teleporter a few days ago."

"I am so glad she knows. I thought I had to develop a story dealing with my work in the lab without you."

Garcia took out her work journal and placed a bookmark. She then looked at Karina and gently hugged her.

"Oh girl, when are you due?"

"In four months or so, it's up to the baby."

"Is it a boy or girl?"

"We don't know its gender, but I'm hoping for a girl."

"Of course, she is while I am hoping for a boy."

As I chimed in with that statement, I looked at Garcia's notes and calculations. I noticed the other pile of papers with different calculations, notes, and some questions, especially one that jumped right at me.

"How can a person travel through a time portal without detection while another group travels in a different portal simultaneously? Also, how can this feat not disturb or destroy the time continuum?"

"So, what do you think of those calculations we developed?"

I closed my eyes as I moved the papers haphazardly without giving Garcia a clue that I read any of it.

"My excursion to 1974 showed up somewhere in the data, or it left an energy surge or signature, which Garcia noticed. She knew I committed an unauthorized teleport but didn't know the location and time period. Yet, she could detect my solo trip in a different portal by matching the different energy outputs for each portal. Just great!"

I looked at her with amazement and concern.

"How can I slow down Garcia's progress or change the direction of her private investigation?"

I then looked at the extensive work on those little problems that can hinder our future missions.

"This looks great, but I need something else."

"What is it, oh master?"

Garcia smiled as she emphatically bowed toward me.

"Can we track people based on their daily activities, like going to work, the doctor, or their bank activities? You know how Professor Charles Xavier did it in the X-Men comics and movies."

"Yes, we can, but not like Charles Xavier. I can go one better. We can track their whereabouts during their leisure activities as well. It will take some doing, but I will tackle any glitches that may develop."

"Great! I presume we can use the TVU since it has enough juice and capability to do the job."

"Yes, the TVU has been updated for many purposes, which I can exhibit when you return from your sabbatical."

"That's good to know. How soon can you get it up and running?"

"I should have it ready in a couple of hours."

"Good! Now send the program and calculations to me when you can."

I picked up a couple of TVUs, placed them in my backpack, and walked toward Karina as she turned toward my number one lab technician.

"Bye, Garcia. The next time you see me, I will be either in a full batá as large as an elephant or holding my child."

Karina rubbed her belly.

"I hope so, either way."

Garcia smiled.

"Oh, Al, who are you looking for through this new program you want me to develop?"

"An old friend, Garcia."

I turned from her, took my phone out, and pressed the camera app. I returned to Garcia's desk and other tables as if looking for other data sheets. Garcia wasn't concerned about my rummaging because she was laser-focused on her immediate project.

"I am sure she will find out who is my dear old friend after she completes her thorough search of those mysterious energy surges."

I took some photos of Garcia's notes and strange writings while she started the computer setup for the tracking system. I then packed my backpack and satchel full of other tiny gadgets and materials for future projects. I waved at Garcia and took Karina's hand as we walked out of the laboratory to continue our sabbatical for the next three to seven months.

"What is up Garcia's sleeve? Why doesn't she ask me about our 1865 rescue mission?"

I rubbed Karina's hand with my index finger.

"What's gotten into Albert? This is not like him to have secrets. Does Karina know about his secret trip to 1974?"

Garcia looked at the loving couple she greatly admired while working for Albert and NYU.

~

"Bang! Bang!"

I quickly paused the recorder playback and then folded my hands together.

"Dr. Hernandez, where is all of this going? This is not telling us anything about the time continuum and your claim that we need to fix the timeline or how we skewed from the correct and original timeline."

"I understand your frustration Mr. Jones, but this background will show how the timeline shifted and who are the players in this story. These recordings will also show you who is responsible for the many errors and mishaps during our missions. I believe the person or persons behind this ultimate crime are present within these recordings and in this council room."

Karina, Garcia, Corey, and Wilma looked at each other and the rest of our laboratory team. They wondered to themselves who could be the culprit of our time shift.

"Very well, Mr. Hernandez, we will see this through as long as we get concrete answers to our questions and on who committed this time shift."

The Chairman hit his gavel several times to get everyone's attention.

"Ladies and gentlemen, we will continue this testimony until we get a satisfactory answer to Dr. Hernandez's claims of time shifting."

My team and Robinson's team were the only two groups of people present during the hearing. I looked at them as many encouraged me to continue my testimony with a nod, a thumbs up, and a few encouraging words like the following.

"You got this, boss!" Wilma yelled.

"Yeah, what she said. We're behind you, Al!" Corey said.

"Bang! Bang!"

"Ok, ladies and gentlemen, let's settle down so we can proceed with this hearing."

I got up, approached the playback machine, and then pressed play.

~

Garcia went back to her work, which was three-pronged. First, she continued with her work on improving the Teleporter specs for future missions. Second, she continued with her investigation of my ill-advised trip to 1974, and thirdly, to complete the assignment I gave her dealing with calculations on locating individuals anywhere on the earth.

Chapter 32

November 22, 2021– 10:23 PM

"Buzz, Buzz!"

My Time Viewer Unit vibrated for a few minutes during the wee hours of the evening, approximately 10:23 PM. I stumbled out of bed and grabbed the device from my bureau. I looked for my glasses and found them on top of my head. I chuckled and then shook my head to get rid of the cobwebs. The blurred text message became more apparent after I put on my reading glasses, and not surprisingly, it was from Garcia.

"Al, here are the calculations and sequences for locating a person in our present and the pat. This can be useful for future missions and trips through time. Good luck, and I hope you find your friend. Good night."

Incredibly, Garcia is so friendly and secretive simultaneously. I hope she asks me about my excursion trip to my past.

"Thanks, Garcia. I'll let you know what turns up in my search. Good night my friend."

I examined the equations, took off my glasses, and then looked at Karina after she shifted from one side of the bed to the other. Her arm reached my side, anticipating my body there, but she came up empty. She raised her head, looking for me.

"Al, please come back and finish massaging my back and legs."

"In one minute, sweetie."

I tested the calculations and then looked at my Apple Watch: 10:45 PM.

"Now I can insert the program into the teleporter operation system and locate Coach Hood," I said to myself.

It took five minutes for the program to pinpoint and map Coach Hood's location.

"He is at home within the borough of Manhattan along the West 10s. He's been near NYU all this time, and, amazingly, I haven't bumped into him these past four years."

I shook my head and rubbed my face, trying to wipe away the shock. I shut down my TVU, joined Karina at our king-size bed, and continued massaging her back.

"What is it, honey?"

"I can't believe I'm going to track down my abuser so I can preach to him about Jesus Christ. It sounds crazier when I say it out loud."

I finished massaging my love and then looked at my TVU for a few more minutes.

"Al, we are all lost until we accept Jesus as our personal Savior. Coach Hood needs to hear he has a chance for salvation."

"Before I do that, I must return to that time period. I need to look at something I believe I missed or misunderstood."

"What are you looking for?"

"Hope!"

I went to my side of the bed, turned towards my night table, shut off the lamp, and then spooned my lovely and understanding wife. We went to sleep peacefully.

~

November 23, 2021– 9:47 AM

The lab door slid open.

"Good morning, Garcia."

I entered the lab and walked towards her.

"Al, what are you doing here?"

She quickly organized her papers.

"I work here, duh!"

"Yeah, of course you do, but you have taken a sabbatical and are not due for a few months. You also said you need to settle old matters. So, have you settled that old score?"

"No, I haven't because I need to do something else before I 'settle that old score,' as you put it."

I placed a pumpkin spice muffin on the teleporter's console before her.

"Really? Do you believe a food bribe will get you what you need from me? If you resort to this tactic, it must be serious and possibly not approved by Agent Robinson or the agency. What do you need from me?"

Garcia moved the muffin to her desk and then looked at her computer screen.

"Garcia, I need to go to the past to gather information concerning my old friend and see whether it's worth settling a particular situation between us."

"What info and how far in the past? You know we have had issues with the time portal since our last mission."

"Yeah, I know, but I have an equation that may overcome those portal issues and allow me to travel without a hitch to the proper destination points in my journey. So, don't you worry. I got it covered. As for the time period, you will see where I am going once I get through the portal. The info is personal and has affected me for many years. I must do this for my soul and the person I found through your calculations last night. Thanks, by the way."

Garcia nodded. I started to walk towards the teleporter chamber.

"Wait a minute!"

Garcia walked towards me. I thought she would stop me, but that was not the case. She reluctantly handed me a small key chain that contained the sequence needed to link my TVU to the teleporter.

"Thanks, Garcia. I will never forget this."

I clicked the key chain to a larger key ring on my belt. I entered the chamber, took my TVU from my satchel, flipped it to its screen, and pressed one green button and then a red button to start my journey.

"Zap!"

I was gone in seconds. Garcia turned on her TVU with the sequence she gave me, which was embedded into her device to trace my movements through time. This was one of the new programs to help monitor our travels through the portal away from the Teleporter.

"I truly hope he finds what he is looking for?"

I looked at my device.

"Man, I am moving faster than I did during our last mission. Garcia made improvements in the teleporter's energy transfer unit. I can quickly return to my youth and see who I was before my abuse."

Lord Lead Me

by Heaven's Choir

Throughout my life, I wandered through the wilderness
  There was an endless road leading to nowhere
  There was no light to see ahead
  There were only noises of gnashing teeth and screams
  around me
  Where can I go to escape this scene and find peace?
  I just want to speak to You, my God.

<u>Chorus</u>
Lord, I need You to light the way
Lord help me to deal with my trials and tribulation
I have doubts and anguish
Please quench my fears
You are the only One Who can rescue me from my mess
So Lord Lead me!

After being abused with no recollection
I have lived an angry life
My heart full of heart brought me to make the
wrong decisions

I was still lost even though I had many worldly successes
There was no peace in my heart
I took in a drink or two instead of crying out to You

<u>Chorus</u>
Lord, I need You to light the way
Lord, help me to deal with my trials and tribulation
I have doubts and anguish
Please quench my fears
You are the only One Who can rescue me from my mess
So Lord Lead me!

Once I believed in You and what You have done for me
A joy slowly crept into my heart
Do I deserve such peace?
I went to sleep, and You showed me an answer to my
constant question
Why was I always angry?
You revealed that I was abused during my youth
"Lord after saving me why show me my ugly past?"
And the answer was clear
"I didn't want you to end your life and spend eternity in
Hell.
You belong to Me."
I was astounded by my Lord's precious protection.
I love You Lord forever!

<u>Chorus</u>
Lord, I need You to light the way
Lord, help me to deal with my trials and tribulation
I have doubts and anguish
Please quench my fears
You are the only One Who can rescue me from my mess
So Lord Lead me!

Chapter 33

31 AD

The quick trip through the portal brought a rapid entry to what I thought was my youth. Instead, it was another time period that I didn't recognize. I materialized within a grand city. The people and their clothes clued me into their Middle Eastern area and possible time period. I hoped my garb didn't bring much attention to me and my circumstance. I pulled out my TVU after taking cover in an alleyway. My device showed,

31 AD – The Healing at Bethesda within Jerusalem

I punched in a sequential equation to test and use for exiting the time period I had just entered so I could reach my original destination – my youth's time period. The TVU stated,

"No access to the time portal you requested at this time."

I shook my head.

"I can't believe it. I thought we overcame McGee's interference?"

I put the TVU away and decided to look around Jerusalem. It took only a few minutes to find Jesus talking to a crippled man. He said to him,

"Do you want to get well?"

The sick man answered Him,

"Sir, I have no man to put me into the pool when the water is stirred up, but while I am coming, another steps down before me."

Jesus said to him,

"Get up, pick up your pallet and walk."

Immediately the man became well and picked up his pallet, and began to walk. I got closer to Jesus as the healed man walked right by me.

"I see you have returned. So will you forgive Coach Hood or hold on to your anger?"

I was stunned by His question. How can Jesus from 31AD know about Coach Hood and my problem with him?

"Lord, I actually entered time to investigate the genesis of Hood's behavior and what kind of boy I was before the abuse."

Jesus began to walk away from the Bethesda Pool and headed towards the temple.

"Al, Coach Hood is a troubled soul and is suffering tremendously. He desperately wants to be cleansed from his sins and forgiven. He needs forgiveness from you and Me, which will give him a new beginning. Al, you know what I am talking about? Being born again."

"Lord, I want to investigate further. I am not planning to hurt him."

"In the depths of your heart, you still want to kill him. You have tremendous hate for him."

I looked down and away due to my shame.

"Yes, I dreamt of killing him, but I realized that he matters to You and that You love him as much as You love me. So, I want to forgive and help him if possible."

"Sounds good, Al. Before you go, I want to tell you something about your mission."

"Ok, Lord, what is it?"

"You need to finish your planned research and forgive Coach Hood before you attempt to fix the time continuum."

"Ok, Lord, I will research and try to reach Coach Hood before he hurts others. I hope I have enough time to complete these missions."

"Beep!"

I quickly took out my TVU and read its screen,

"Follow the healed man."

"Is today a Sabbath day?"

"Yes, Al, it is. Now, look at their disdain for what I did."

So the Jews were saying to the man who was cured,

"It is a Sabbath, and it is not permissible for you to carry your pallet."

But he answered them,

"He who made me well was the one who said to me, 'Pick up your pallet and walk.'"

They asked him,

"Who is the man who said to you, 'Pick it up and walk'?"

The man looked for Jesus and was not able to find Him until within the Temple. Jesus said to him,

"Behold, you have become well; do not sin anymore so that nothing worse happens to you."

The man went away and informed the Jews that it was Jesus who had made him well. For this reason, the Jews were persecuting Jesus because He was doing these things on the Sabbath. But He answered them,

"My Father is working until now, and I Myself am working."

I stood near Jesus while witnessing those exchanges until I heard a wonderful sound.

"Beep!"

I took out my TVU and looked at its screen. It stated,

"Time portal is ready for entry."

I looked toward Jesus and waved at Him. He waved back and said,

"Remember to follow My Voice."

The portal sucked me in without warning, and I almost lost my TVU, cell phone, and another small gadget from my hands and satchel.

"Zip!"

Chapter 34

2242 BC

I landed upon a dune near a developing city. After recovering from my rapid trip, I took out my TVU and pressed a few buttons to find where I had landed. My TVU screen stated the following,

2242 BC – The Tower of Babel

I found many people walking towards and away from the city. Once I entered the city, I saw the people busy at work completing the construction of the city walls, different buildings, and a sizeable incomplete tower. I noticed everyone was speaking the same language. Then they said to one another,

"Come, let's make bricks and burn them thoroughly."

And they used brick for stone, and they used tar for mortar. And they said,

"Come, let's build ourselves a city and a tower whose top will reach into heaven, and let's make a name for ourselves; otherwise, we will be scattered abroad over the face of all the earth."

I quickly walked away from that group. And the Lord said,

"Behold, they are one people, and they all have the same language. And this is what they have started to do, and now nothing which they plan to do will be impossible for them. Come, let Us go down and there confuse their language so that they will not understand one another's speech."

I heard the Lord clearly as if I was listening to Karina's explanation of some historical fact.

So the Lord scattered them abroad from there over the face of all the earth, and they stopped building the city. Therefore it was named Babel because the Lord confused the language of all the earth, and from there, the Lord scattered them abroad over the face of all the earth. I hid behind a large wall to avoid being trampled by a large stampede of people. Fear and confusion were evident on their faces as they tried to communicate with each other. They were confused by how they spoke different languages just seconds after understanding each other. Secondly, they were fearful of Who or What this sudden change in their speech was. Were they able to ascertain that God was behind their sudden language change?

"Beep!"

I took out my TVU while the rumbling of the stampede continued around me. The Time Viewer Unit screen stated,

"Green light for your travel through the portal!"

I pressed the flashing green button, instantly shifted into the portal, and flew through it towards May 3, 1974.

"Zap!"

Of course, I hoped that was true.

Chapter 35

No Time – Within the Time Portal (Sent out through time from November 22, 2021, and entered June 24, 1972 – 2:30 PM)

"What will I find when I exit the portal? Will I enter the designated time period this time? Which day of the year did I select, or did I? I didn't specify the time; instead, I used the roulette program, so I don't know or anticipate the events that will unfold once I enter it. I want to discover what kind of life I was living before I crossed paths with Coach Hood."

I observed the different historical events flashing across the time portal walls. I couldn't make most of them due to the speed I traveled through the portal. Then, a sudden flash occurred, and the portal shook. I saw my life unfold along those walls, and a grey figure passed me.

"What was that? Was it a person, or was it a ghost? Is this the second or third time I have seen that shadowy figure?"

My movements through the portal began to slow down, which signaled my exit from it and my entrance into an undescriptive time period. After I landed next to a baseball field, I saw a group of kids playing softball on a cloudless day. Within minutes, I saw myself standing beside a makeshift home plate with my bat on my shoulder. I swung my bat several times, gearing up for what the pitcher would throw at me. The pitch came in swiftly, and my younger counterpart smashed the ball over the centerfield wall. It was a grand slam, and the team won. My younger counterpart jumped on Homeplate after circling the baseball diamond.

"Wow! I was thrilled and carefree."

I grew angry at the sight of my glee and normalcy. I pressed the green button on my TVU, and in a flash, I teleported seven months into the future. I tumble into my old neighborhood, which was in the suburbs of LA. I noticed a Ferris wheel, booths with various games, and other rides for younger kids. It was our neighborhood street fair. I saw my younger counterpart being timid and unsure while attempting to speak to a girl he had been attracted to for some time. After several minutes of coaxing from my father, my younger counterpart approached the young girl and asked her out. She said yes. He kissed her cheek, twirled, and then stood on his toes as Michael Jackson did in one of his dance routines. My younger counterpart then ran to my father, hugged him, and then my father gave my younger counterpart a high five.

I froze at that spot. I was stunned by the sight of my father, looking young, strong, and healthy. It was incredible that his death was within twelve years or so from that moment in my personal history. I was stunned at how he looked since I hadn't seen him for years, since his death. Tears flowed down my cheeks as I shook off a sudden wave of grief within the depths of my soul.

"Daddy, I want to run to you and hug you, but I know I can't."

I suddenly hid behind a group of people. I squeezed my eyes shut as more tears flowed down my cheeks. Another memory of my dad came roaring back.

~

My Dad loved baseball and never missed a Dodger home opener, except during his cancer years. He took my brother and me to one of those season openers when I was ten. I remembered our seat location and how cool it was that day. We sat in the nosebleed section and couldn't read the player's name on their jerseys unless we used his binoculars. We had a great time. It was one of the few moments we had with no yelling, arguments, spanking, or hitting. I also loved baseball, and him for taking me to those games.

~

Once that memory vanished as vapor, I looked towards heaven and asked God for comfort and wisdom during my present journey.

"Help me, Lord. What am I doing to myself by coming back to these time periods? This experiment only proves there is only one answer for permanent relief."

I quickly pressed the green button to move a couple of years into the scene of my abuse. I put away the TVU and held on to my gun in my hoodie jacket pocket. I didn't tell anyone, not even Karina, that I would kill Coach Hood and end this constant pain. I exited the time portal into the area in front of the boy's locker room. Once again, I entered the locker room and heard physical movements from one of the bathroom stalls. I ran to it and slowly reached for the doorknob when a strong wind rushed between me and the door. I dropped the gun as I fell back. I looked up to find a faceless grey figure. I looked closer and discovered that the figure was wearing a grey mask. I had to find out why this figure was here.

"Who are you?"

"Listen to the Lord. He will lead you to the truth and the correct path. Only he can repair the pain and anguish in your heart."

"I need to stop this tragic event from escaping this cycle of pain I've been suffering."

"No. Only Jesus can rescue you from this abusive cycle. You must have faith in Him or be stuck in this cycle forever."

"Who are you? Are you an angel?"

"Remember what I said, 'Only Jesus can rescue you from this cycle.'"

"Whoosh!"

The grey figure left me with the most critical decision in my life.

"I am always with you no matter what you did or are about to do, but one road will be far more difficult in your travels than the other. My Son has provided the Grace and Way to salvation through His death and resurrection. You can either give up this plan, repent of your internal evil thoughts, and follow Him closely, or fulfill your plan and suffer the consequences of your actions, which is God's Wrath. If you choose to kill Coach Hood, then you will have a difficult road with only one way to get salvation – believing that Jesus is the Son of God. He died on the cross for all of your sins, rose from the dead, and is seated at the right hand of Father God. Of course, you will ask for forgiveness of all your sins, but you need to surrender all transgressions

in action and thought and turn away from those transgressions – in other words, Repent! This second road of repentance is more difficult without Me, so lean on Me. Al, killing Coach Hood will also change history and the time continuum," a peaceful, low-audible voice stated.

I picked up my gun, rose, raised my head towards heaven, and prayed.

"Father, I have accepted Jesus Christ as my Savior and want to scare Coach Hood. I want him to beg for mercy and ask for forgiveness. At that moment, I will decide what to do."

I wondered whether I was doing the right thing or tempting evil into my heart. Coach Hood entered the bathroom area, and I quickly cornered him. I pointed my gun at him with the barrel aimed right between his eyes.

"Now, you will pay for the pain you gave me. This will erase the agony I suffered for all of these years!"

I shouted as I stood frozen as an immovable statue with my gun fixed on my prey. He went down to his knees.

"Please don't shoot. Whatever I did to you was inexcusable. I couldn't help it. I am sick."

"Your words will not change anything."

I placed my finger on the trigger. I squeezed the trigger slowly as if time slowed to a virtual stop. Coach Hood lowered his head, anticipating and bracing for the shot. Suddenly, my younger counterpart jumped out of the bathroom stall and ran out. I jumped from fright, but at the same time, I felt a nudge from a black figure on my right side.

"Bang! Bang!"

My gun went off, and Coach Hood crumbled to the moist ground. I stood there for several seconds, stunned by what had transpired. The black figure stood there for a few seconds until the familiar grey figure chased it out of the bathroom. I then ran out as kids and adults rushed in. I raced down the hallway with my head down, trying to avoid any eye contact as I pressed the green button on my device when I exited the building. I was catapulted into the time portal with my gun still in my hand. I quickly wiped it and placed it in my satchel with the safety on. I turned towards the portal walls, looking for any historical changes.

"I'm still empty. I thought I would be elated or free from the anguish. Instead, I feel more fear than ever and am now guilty of what I did. It doesn't seem that this timeline has changed. Maybe he was just wounded from the gunfire and recovered. I hope so. I can't believe I hope for my abuser to survive his wound. My heart must be changing."

I took out my TVU to scan the timeline, but it didn't respond to my request. It just showed one time period – Jesus' birth. I shook my head and put my device into my satchel.

"I can't believe I shot Coach Hood. Something or someone bumped into me to cause my gun to go off. I hope I didn't kill him. What has happened to me? I wanted him dead and to be free from the pain he caused, but I just wanted this pain to die. So far, the events on the portal walls seem the same as before, but my TVU would have to verify whether it is still working properly."

I covered my face due to guilt and despair at this new situation, and suddenly, a peaceful memory flooded my mind.

~

"I was ten years old and was walking through a crowd as I held on to my mother and father's hands. It was a sunny, cloudless summer day with a light breeze. I heard many people screaming from a distance. At first, I was scared of those screams, but as I looked around, I realized people were on some twirling ride and Ferris wheel on the Santa Monica Pier. I smiled in glee with the hope of experiencing such fright and joy simultaneously. I felt a salty breeze hitting my face and the freshness of that cool air on such a hot day. I just wanted to open my mouth and gulp it all in. I looked up to see my parents smiling and laughing while my two brothers and two sisters were bothering each other as usual. We reached Nathans, and my father ordered hot dogs, fries, and soda for the whole family. He brought the large tray of food to our table. We each had two hot dogs, a cup of fries, and soda."

~

The tears on my face dried up and were replaced with a smile.

"I truly miss those days."

I Need You

by The Lord's Dominion

Lord, please do not leave me. I need You every day
> You are the Creator, and I am the created
> You are sovereign
> While I am Your servant
> Am I worthy of being Yours?
> Only Your Son's blood can rescue me
> Even though I accepted Your Son as my Savior
> My actions must reflect my submission to You, my Lord God.

<u>Chorus</u>
I need You more than ever, my Lord
I will run every day to You
I will run for You
I will run to hear You
I will run to speak to You
I will run from evil and into Your arms, my Lord
So today, I submit my life to You, my Lord
This is not my life to live but Yours to serve
So today, I submit my life to You, my Lord
This is not my life to live but Yours to serve

Oh Lord, remove this heart of stone and selfishness
And replace it with a heart of flesh and selflessness
<u>Chorus</u>
I need You more than ever, my Lord
I will run every day to You
I will run for You
I will run to hear You
I will run to speak to You
I will run from evil and into Your arms, my Lord
So today, I submit my life to You, my Lord
This is not my life to live but Yours to serve

Oh Lord, give me the Wisdom to confound the self-righteous
And a patient spirit to speak the Truth
May Your Words teach me how to follow You, my Lord
And imitate You, my Jesus
<u>Chorus</u>
I need You more than ever, my Lord
I will run every day to You
I will run for You
I will run to hear You
I will run to speak to You
I will run from evil and into Your arms, my Lord
So today, I submit my life to You, my Lord
This is not my life to live but Yours to serve

Lord, please do not remove the Holy Spirit from my life
Please help me with my sinful nature and weakness to stave off my lust
You are the Redeemer, my Lord
And I humble myself to You and worship Your mighty Name
I open the door of my heart
Please enter and control my life

Chapter 36

November 2, 2021– 10:33 PM

The teleporter chamber hummed back to life as light flashes filled the container and quickly shot into the laboratory. Many sparkling little lights appeared, and then I materialized. I slowly stepped out of the chamber, full of anxiety and guilt, as I pushed back my hood.

"Hey, that was quick Al. Did you complete your mission? Did you get the intel you needed to settle your old score?"

"Yes and no, Garcia."

I looked at the pictures of Karina on my desk.

"It's amazing how she was right on how I am supposed to handle my past. I might have made a mistake that could change my life and possibly alter some part of history. Yet, I am unsure whether the shooting was accidental."

"What?"

"Never mind, Garcia. I have to go now."

I left the lab without another word.

"Oh, ok? See you later."

Garcia looked closely at the teleporter's specs and extrapolated my different positions as I traveled through the portal. Garcia turned to the Time Viewer and rewound the previous historical events. The Viewer can replay significant and insignificant events. She then played it forward as she looked closely for anything unusual. Garcia saw my image entering

May 3rd, 1974, and walking to a locker room's bathroom area. She saw the gun and then, "Bang!" Garcia brought her hand to her mouth in shock.

"Why would Al kill that man? Hold on."

She saw a grey figure moving within that room and a dark figure standing next to me, and then they both disappeared as if one were chasing the other.

"I need to see what happened."

She rewound the video, slowly replayed the scene several times, and examined it frame by frame.

"Wow! I can't believe it. Should I tell Al about this or …," Garcia asked herself.

She then looked at the timeline specs on the computer screen.

"Now that's interesting. Does Karina know anything about this event or what Al planned to do at that time period? How can I take advantage of this new development?"

Garcia smiled with glee.

November 22, 2021– 10:43 PM

Robinson got into his car and put on his listening sensor app.

"What is she saying?"

He increased the volume. He heard paper moving from one area to another and the rigid tapping whenever she hit a key on her computer.

"Did he really do that? I can't believe Al can do that," Garcia whispered.

"What is Garcia talking about?" Robinson thought as he increased the sensor's volume.

Suddenly, his sensor went dead. He tapped his phone a couple of times and was unsuccessful. Robinson heard only buzzing and crackling through his phone speaker. He closed down the app, started his car, and drove off.

"What did Albert commit? Was it a crime or an unauthorized trip to the past? I will get my techs to look into the teleporter data for the past three days. Al and his team think I can't keep up with their tech savviness, but I will surprise them in a few months."

Robinson sped through the Manhattan traffic, entered the 59th Street Bridge, and drove into Queens for the evening. He smiled.

"Oh, they will be wondering what hit them."

November 22, 2021– 11:32 PM

"Sweetie, I need to look at some data and specs dealing with our recent mission."

I got up from our bed, grabbed my satchel and two journals from my night table, and exited the bedroom.

"Ok, babe. Don't be surprised you find me asleep."

Karina started a video game on her iPad.

"If you say so. Then I must say goodnight right now."

I smiled as I went to her and gave her a goodnight kiss. I quickly extracted myself from the bedroom before I was hooked into another conversation with her and walked to my study.

"I need to know what caused my gun to go off. Was it me? Was it a supernatural force? Was it someone else from the future? Or did the gun malfunction and fired off on its own?"

I placed the TVU on my desk and pulled out a medium black case from one of the desk drawers. I unzipped the case and rolled out a velvet casing to reveal small tools. I used two types of screwdrivers and one tiny plier to remove the back cover of the TVU. I adjusted the speed of the historical playback and changed the accuracy of each event request, whether historically based or personal. I reattached the back cover and screwed it tight, and then turned the TVU around to look at its screen. I was able to retrieve the day on which I went back to confront Coach Hood. I saw my younger counterpart in the bathroom being lured into the stall. After a few minutes, my younger counterpart jumped out of the stall as I stood at its entrance, confronting Coach Hood. I saw myself pointing my gun toward Coach Hood. My gun went off within seconds or a few minutes, and I just stood there stunned.

"It's not clear. I cannot make out what happened in that small bathroom area."

I announced loud for all to hear, but no one was present to hear it. I rewound the video and played it in the slowest speed setting. I could make out an image or figure that moved right next to me and bumped into me. I couldn't tell whether the figure was a man or a woman. I pushed off my desk and nearly slammed into the wall behind me; instead, my chair slid from its upright position, and I landed on the hardwood floor. I got up and then texted Karina.

"Sorry about the loud noise. I fell off my chair — no need for you to come by the study. I am all right. Good night, Sweetie."

As I regained my composure on my chair, I looked at my Time Viewer Unit and noticed that I could not find Coach Hood in the present time period. I frantically entered every fact I knew about Coach Hood, and the TVU indicated that no such person existed in any time period. At that moment, I knew I had returned to the lab and gathered my gear for a new mission – to find out who killed Coach Hood and correct that tragic event. Yet, the Teleporter is out of commission for the next seven months, and by then, I would have to find out which portal I entered, leading me to this unexpected tragedy. I returned to my bedroom to find Karina fast asleep in front of her iPad. I carefully took her tablet, rolled her blanket over her body, and kissed her forehead. I went to my bathroom to wash up for the evening. I looked at my reflection.

"History has changed, and I'm not sure the events we're living out right now are the correct timeline for all mankind."

Chapter 37

May 2, 2022– 10 PM

I ensured Karina was comfortably lying in bed with our baby in her womb. She had a slightly difficult pregnancy for the most part, but it was pain-free for the past four weeks. Afterward, I gave her a back and tummy massage, and she enjoyed a warm bath. Within 21 minutes, she was fast asleep. I took this opportunity to take my satchel and other materials related to the teleporter and our past mission to our office. I brought over notebooks, diagrams, graphs, and recordings of our last mission.

It had been six months since I last tried looking up Coach Hood. I took out my TVU and laptop to examine and test Garcia's equations and calculations to locate individuals worldwide based on their name, racial nationality, gender, height, weight, and approximate age. My three attempts came up empty. Each entry indicated that Coach Hood never existed. I was shocked by that result because I thought history would show that he had a life until he was shot in that bathroom stall. Instead, it seems that Coach Hood had been erased from history by the accidental murder I witnessed on my last teleporter trip.

While I looked at my laptop and TVU screens, I wondered whether I should try to bring Coach Hood back from his unforeseen death. Yet, whether it was done by me or someone else, I'm grateful he is gone. For thirty years, I have been haunted by his gleaming teeth and foul, smelly clothes. I awoke from nightmares of that dreadful day, seemingly trapped in the darkened bathroom stall. The remembrances of how he grabbed and violated me overwhelmed any memories of my youthful innocence.

Can I ever get my youth back? Can I ever return to those beautiful crisp blue sky days and the gentle breeze caressing my face? They seem so unreachable today. I suffered from anxiety, panic attacks, and constant fear of men through the years. Since I first met Karina, she told me I always seemed melancholy, like there was no joy or underlying happiness. I am only happy when I bring joy to others. Don't get me wrong; I remember glimpses of my youth when I was innocent and joyful before 12 years old. Can those feelings and state of mind ever come back? It's like an unreachable or unattainable joy. Karina and one of my brothers, Paul, told me that I might have an arrested youth makeup, meaning that I have never grown up to a certain maturity regarding my emotional and mental state. It's like I am perpetually trapped in this cycle of a preteen state of mind. This may be similar to being trapped in a time vortex. Suddenly, a prayer and thought entered my heart and mind.

"Even though Coach Hood was killed either by me or by one of the figures I saw in my last mission, I am still lost with myself. So, erasing Coach Hood didn't bring me back to who I was before that terrible incident. Now I wonder whether this timeline is correct, so I performed many tests through my TVU and laptop to find that we were on the wrong time continuum. Lord, I cannot fulfill what You wanted me to do in dealing with Coach Hood's salvation. I have eliminated him, either directly or indirectly. I need to fix this, but how can I do it? I may need help from Garcia and Corey to fix this gross error. This timeline is incorrect, but how can I convince anyone that we must fix this? Everyone would think this is the correct timeline. Lord, I need your help in this dilemma."

I stood there waiting for God to answer, but there was nothing. I picked up my cell phone and pressed the speed dial button.

"Hey, Al, what's up?"

"Hola, Garcia. I know you are home relaxing for once, but I need you to assemble the team."

"The entire team, boss?"

"No, you're right. The whole team is not needed. Just get Wilma and Corey."

"Are you ok, Al?"

I ignored her question because I didn't want to break down and reveal my secret.

"I'll bring Karina to our meeting. We should rendezvous at my lab at 0900 hours."

"Got it, Al. What's the plan?"

"We need to fix something that has been broken for several years," I whispered.

"What?"

"Never mind. We'll see you and the team at 0900 hours sharp. Rest up and goodnight."

I returned to my TVU and computer to plug in my experiments and attempt to reach Coach Hood. I also used that time to formulate a detailed plan to change that dreadful event. I worked on the recovery project for many hours until I fell asleep at my desk. Karina came in and nudged me, and said,

"Honey, let's get you to bed. You have worked tirelessly on this problem for months. You must surrender it to God and let Him work on it."

"Yes, sweetie, I will do that, but I messed up. Will God help me even though I still have hatred toward Coach Hood? I may want this to happen so I can forget the physical and mental pain he brought upon me," I mumbled, half asleep.

We sauntered to our bedroom; I changed into my PJs and quickly fell asleep, dreaming of ways to fix the tragic shift in our time continuum.

Chapter 38

May 3, 2022– 9 AM

The lab door slid open as Karina and I walked into the lab. Karina was larger than ever, with our child moving within her uterus. Garcia smiled at the sight of her motherly condition and quickly presented a chair for her.

"Thanks, Garcia. The walk from our car was dreadful, even though we were parked in front of the building."

"I'm sure it was, but why didn't you stay home and rest? We got this girl."

"It's ok. I want to help fix this error."

"What error, Karina?"

"Hey Garcia, do you have the Teleporter ready for travel?"

"Yes, sir. It's ready but with no destination."

"I'll give it to you after I brief the team. In fact, where are Wilma and Corey?"

"They texted me that they were on their way back. They went out to get some goodies. I'm sure you guys are hungry."

"Of course, you always said that a mission is never fueled on an empty stomach."

On cue, Cory and Wilma entered the lab with bags of food. The aroma streamed throughout the lab, which caused my stomach to rumble.

"Ok, guys, break out the grub. I'll explain our mission while we enjoy this fine meal."

"Now you're talking, Al," Wilma smiled.

After a half hour of eating our breakfast and small talk, I got up and turned to the group.

"Guys, I must reveal something I did during our last mission."

"Al, what did you do that required us to be here this morning? We were all together during the entire mission. We would have noticed any action that may have been contrary to the mission."

"Well, Corey, I committed an unauthorized trip to 1974."

"What?"

"Why?"

"Ok, hold on. Let me explain."

"Did your trip affect our timeline?"

"I'll get to that, Corey, after I explain why I did the trip in the first place."

I told them what Coach Hood did to me when I was 12 years old, what I wanted to do to change that event, and the circumstances that followed. For a minute or two, Corey, Wilma, and Garcia were stunned by a heavy silence. I looked at each person with careful measure. Corey rubbed his head as he walked around the lab. Wilma stared expressionless at the Teleporter while Garcia looked at her computer screen and notes.

"Well, guys? What questions do you have for me?"

"Al, this explains what you did during the mission, but not about your second trip into that time period. What happened during that trip, and how did it affect our timeline?"

I looked at Garcia, and right at that moment, I realized she knew what had happened during my second trip.

"Somehow, she could hear or view the events in that bathroom."

I lowered my head in shame.

"Yes, Garcia, I went back to scare my abuser so that he won't do it again to someone else. Instead, it went sideways."

"Really Al? Trying to scare him with a gun was not wise at all!"

"Honey, what did you do?"

"Like I was trying to say. I took my gun to scare Coach Hood, but it went off. I saw him crumble to the floor and die."

"What?"

"Al, you have changed the timeline!"

"First of all, Corey, I believed I didn't because I discovered that Coach Hood had no significance to add or subtract from any historical event. Yet…"

"He did in some way, didn't he?"

"I believe so, Wilma, because I can't find a trace of his existence before he was killed. It's as if there was never a Coach Hood in my Middle School or his neighborhood, even though I still remember him."

"Hold on. Are we living in a different timeline?"

"Yes, I believe so."

"Now you want us to fix it before this timeline grows further than it is and before it reaches a point that we won't be able to fix at all?"

"Well, Garcia, two of us will go back to 1974, before the shooting, and try to prevent Coach Hood's murder while I need the two of you to observe the sequence of events within that bathroom, looking for anything that led to his murder as well as who committed the murder."

Every team member looked at each other with great concern.

"Ok, Al, I'll only do this to ensure we live through the correct timeline, but we shouldn't keep secrets from each other."

"Agree, Corey. Are you all in agreement with my plan?"

Each of them gave an affirmative reply. I saw Karina looking at me as if she didn't know me. She got up and went to my office. I immediately followed her.

"Al, where are you going? We need to get the Teleporter set up for your trip. Also, who will travel with you?"

I quickly told her what she should do while attending to my wife. Garcia nodded and got the rest of the team into action. I reached my office and found Karina at my desk, staring at our picture at Restaurant Row. We were delighted that day with great joy for the future. Karina looked at me with a few tears streaming down her cheek with her arms folded across her chest.

"Kari, please forgive me for hiding my erroneous decision to travel to 1974 in my attempt to solve my issues dealing with Coach Hood as I did."

"Al, we agreed never to hide anything from each other when we decided to work on the Teleporter because it's the power of time travel and the possibility of changing time events or total historical records."

"Yes, Kari, we did, and I am sorry for breaking that promise. I don't excuse my actions. I hope you can understand where I was coming from dealing with the hurt, anguish, and shame I continually feel due to Coach Hood's actions. From now on, I will run any idea or decision through you so we can agree on what should be done."

"Al, I do forgive you, but it does hurt. Please don't hurt me again."

"Yes, of course, sweetie."

I rushed to her and hugged her firmly for many minutes, which seemed like an eternity. Garcia saw our embrace and paused during her work.

"I should be his wife. How can that ever happen with her still in the picture?"

Chapter 39

May 3, 2022 – 10:21 AM to May 3, 1974 – 3:30 PM

After entering the Teleporter chamber, Corey and I checked each other's gear and our checklist before the original time portal entry countdown. Once we completed the checklists, I gave Garcia the thumbs up to commence the countdown to our new mission. She nodded, pressed a few buttons, turned two knobs, and moved three levers. The machine came to life, which quickly opened the time portal.

"Zap!"

We got sucked into the portal, which looked very violent, but we experienced a quick, smooth transition from the present time to a space with no time.

"I hope they find the real murderer or stop that dreadful event."

Karina said more to herself than to any person within the lab.

We zoomed through the portal so quickly that the wall images were blurred. Then, without warning, we broke through the portal wall and into our designated time period – May 3, 1974. We landed on a sizeable buffy mat in a middle school gym.

"Corey, are you ok?"

"Yeah, I'm fine. How about you?"

"I'll live. Now let's make sure Coach Hood does as well."

I showed the image of Coach Hood on my TVU screen. It was good that I took his pic before he was murdered since it's the only evidence of his existence. We carefully removed the large stack of mats without causing an avalanche on the gym floor. Corey tracked for Coach Hood while I tracked for my younger counterpart through our respective TVUs. I programmed our devices with the facial recognition program Garcia and Robinson used through the FBI.

Yes, I received permission from the Agency and the President himself to use it for any mission. We just needed to point the device to each person we encountered to match the image we submitted to the program. Unfortunately, many kids and adults were flowing through the hallways of my former middle school, so we stationed ourselves at one of the main internal quads. This is one area that everyone would have to eventually pass through to get to any other part of the school.

"Ping! Ping!"

"I got your coach, Al."

"Good. I got little Albert."

"Now what?"

"Follow Coach Hood, and I'll follow my younger counterpart. They will lead us to the gym and then the locker room. We will rendezvous over there."

"Will do, Al."

We weaved through the various hallways as we followed our respective targets. They entered the gym at different times. My younger counterpart went to the locker room, changed, and left the area to attend the workout with his track team, while Coach Hood joined his assistant coach in his office and went over the day's workout. The assistant coach went out and organized the team for their workout. My younger counterpart entered the cafeteria, walked to the gym, and then to the locker room so he could put away his sweatshirt. It was warmer than he thought at the time. As I entered the cafeteria, I kept an appropriate distance behind my younger counterpart. Coach Hood entered the locker room and approached my younger counterpart. They spoke for a couple of minutes. I motioned Corey to follow me.

"Where is your younger counterpart?"

"He went to the gym but told my former coach that he would return in five minutes."

We moved to the bathroom with our TVUs hidden in our jackets.

"Well, whatever was going on, we must be in that bathroom before they enter it."

"Ok, Al."

We weaved through the flow of students within the hallway between the cafeteria and locker room as they changed classes. It just took us five minutes to traverse the hallway from the cafeteria to the boy's locker room; as I said, it was crowded. I was impressed and concerned that no one noticed two adult males walking through a middle school cafeteria and entering the boy's locker room. It may be that during the last period, many students rushed to leave school for the weekend. Yes, it was Friday, and the buck load of kids wanted to start the weekend as soon as possible.

Once we arrived, we went inside the bathroom and hid in separate stalls. We didn't have to wait that long; Coach Hood and my younger counterpart entered the bathroom. Hood kept on coaxing my younger counterpart into one of the empty stalls. It was good that I guided Corey to a stall further away from the one I was violating. As I listened to the pleading from Hood and the fear in my counterpart, I still couldn't believe I was so naïve and trusting with that wrenched man. Hey, what did I know at 12 years old, especially during 1974, when there was no news of rampant abuse and no internet to publicize it? So, I trusted him with the innocence I had left, which he eventually extracted from my heart. I texted Corey.

"We have to be patient until the grey and black figures appear. We need to see one with a gun and then pounce on them. This means we have to allow the abuse to occur."

"I understand, Al. Wouldn't stopping the abuse prevent those figures from entering this time period?"

"I'm not sure, Corey. This is not the time to experiment with your theory. We need to follow our plan to save Coach Hood's life."

"Ok, Al, you got it."

My older counterpart entered the bathroom, and then suddenly, a bright light appeared from both ends of the bathroom. I looked at the developing scene with great awe.

Chapter 40

Karina, Garcia, and Wilma examined the readings on their respective TVUs, computers, and other sensors connected to the teleporter.

"Ok, guys, how are we going to find out who shot Coach Hood while all of our instruments have indicated that he does not exist?"

"Kari, I have a record of Coach Hood from his youth until 1974."

"How did you get such a record, Garcia? I thought Coach Hood's whole history was erased when he was murdered."

"You're right. Hood's records are erased, but I was able to record all the events Albert experienced when he left for his solo mission. Inadvertently, I asked the computer to record the entire life of Coach Hood, which lasted until May 1974."

"Kari, you should look at it. Fresh eyes may help us find any clues we might have missed towards correcting the time continuum."

Karina walked towards Wilma and whispered,

"Ok, I will do it, Wilma, but questioning Garcia will bring her around towards us dealing with the time continuum. She is giving up on this possibility too easily."

Garcia continued to look through the data given by the teleporter and turned towards Wilma.

"I truly hope you're right, Wilma, but we must focus on the two figures and find their entry point."

Karina reviewed my notes on the time continuum matter and my mini-missions to 1974. She snapped her fingers.

"Ok, guys, let's do this. I'll look at Coach Hood's history until 1974 and monitor Al and Corey's journey while Garcia examines the white figure and Wilma examines the dark figure. What do you think?"

She then walked towards the Teleporter's computer, monitor, and laptop, which contained Hood's history video, to start her review. At the same time, Wilma and Garcia stood beside each other, stunned by Karina's decision.

"Well, I will search these intruders; how about you, Garcia?"

"Yes, I am game."

"Good ladies, let's get to work."

Karina was relieved that either woman did not challenge her assignments.

"Hold on, Kari, I find one thing disturbing about those intruders."

"Oh? What is it, Wilma?"

Wilma walked toward the large TV plasma and pointed toward the two frozen intruders. She then pressed the play button.

"Well, Kari, they seemed to time shift within that period without entering the time portal. I thought you could use only time shift within the portal as you move from one time period to another."

"Really? We should inform Al about your observation; maybe he can look into that later. So, what should you look into regarding your respective intruders – their original location or identities?"

"Well, Kari, we should find their origin and identity."

"Hey Wilma, I will set up the TVUs for both."

"Sounds good, Garcia."

"Yes, I agree, and while you're at that, can you please set up my TVU to trace Coach Hood's history as well and then link the Teleporter to my TVU and iPad to monitor Aland Corey's movements in 1974 and through the time portal?"

"Yeah, Kari, will do. Once I make those changes, I must stay in front of the computer's screen to monitor changes in energy input or output. This will indicate that there are shifts in the time continuum."

"Good. When you discover their origin and identities, please relay your intel to me so I can pass it on to Al. Maybe he can tell us how they are connected to him or our previous mission."

"Looks like we have a plan. Let's hope we can find a way to short-circuit the mysterious figures' mission, which may straighten out our time continuum problem."

"Yeah, I hope so, Wilma, but we may not be successful. Looking for two figures is like looking for two needles in a haystack."

"Hey Garcia, why so negative?"

"Kari, the only way they can be stopped is by entering their time period and physically stopping them. So once we have all this intel, we can either give it to Al or use it and stop those intruders ourselves."

"We will decide after collecting all pertinent data during this mission. Are we in agreement?"

"Yes, Kari," Wilma said.

"Of course, Kari," Garcia said with a sly smile.

"Not unless I make a deal with at least one of them."

Chapter 41

May 3, 1974 – 4:00 PM

"This is not how this scene transpired after I came in. What am I forgetting? Come on, Al, think!" I quietly yelled at myself.

I knew any changes in these events would indeed cause a new lineage of time, and the only remedy was the total erasure of those intruders within this time period.

"Bang! Flash!"

Two bright lights suddenly appeared like small explosions on either side of the bathroom. Corey and I shielded our eyes from the sudden brightness throughout the room. I uncovered my eyes once the brightness subsided. We saw the two figures standing there staring at each other. Masks covered their faces with the same color and texture as their outfits. I looked at Corey, hoping he saw the same thing. Instead, he turned towards me and then shrugged his shoulders.

"Can we get them now, Al?"

"We should get one before the shift reappears within this time period."

Suddenly, my older counterpart entered the scene, which caused the two intruders to flash away from the scene.

"Where did they go?"

"I'm not sure, Corey."

"How can we stop them now?"

"I'm not sure, Corey, but I have a theory."

"Yeah, what is it?"

"We can either speed up this historical time period along with us, so the intruders seem to be traveling at normal speed, or we can slow down their speed by planting this tiny device on them."

I held up a small triangular device with flashing multicolor lights. Corey was able to see the device through my TVU's transmission.

"Al, that was a ridiculous plan you ever developed. How can we do either of them – attachment or activation? We don't have the machinery or programs in our TVUs to do the job."

"Come on, Corey. I have these transmitters."

I took out two pea-sized objects from my TVU. Corey also looked at them through the TVU and shook his head.

"Ok, Al, how can we get those tiny transmitters on those intruders? If we're successful, how can we change their speed or just the speed of this historical time period with our TVUs?"

"Yes, I see your points, and I agree we need something big to trigger the time influx."

"Yeah, man!"

"Hold on, Garcia has the right machine to pull this off."

"I just hope we can reach her in time."

"I'm sure we will. Just have faith."

My older counterpart was recording this developing scene, and I noticed he was carrying a gun. The two figures, one grey, and the other black, reappeared and stood on either side of my older counterpart. They stopped phasing momentarily, and I took the chance and tossed the two gadgets at them. They landed on the backs of both figures. They didn't notice the sudden attachments of those gadgets since they didn't flinch or scratch their backs. I activated the transmitters and set up a link for each through my TVU. I quickly sent the links to Garcia with a note.

"Hey, Garcia, these links are for two devices we developed a few months ago. Please send a high-energy pulse to slow down the two figures. I will explain everything later, so please send the pulses. Thanks, Albert."

"Beep!"

Garcia read the message and quickly sent the links to the Teleporter's computer, then transmitted a beam through the Teleporter to the specific historical time period in 1974, which caused the intruders to slow down. This allowed us to grab them before they could reach the gun in my older counterpart's hand. At the same time, Garcia phased us to a higher speed. The two figures didn't know what hit them.

"Hey, what's happening?" the grey figure said.

"Let go!" the black figure retorted.

Corey and I placed a hockey puck-sized object on our respective intruders. I then activated both disks and sent both figures to their respective historical time periods, countries, and cities.

"Zip!"

The intruders were shocked by their sudden travel out of 1974.

"Hey, Al, what will stop them from doing this again?"

"I implanted the coordinates of the intruder's local law enforcement, and I also encrypted a message for the officer in charge explaining the crime those intruders committed."

"They will get a weird vibe from the package and message."

"Yeah, you're right, but I left Agent Robinson's phone number so they can get verification dealing with my attached message."

I pressed my own TVU's buttons for a return trip home. I then looked at my older counterpart doing the same as my younger counterpart ran out of the bathroom stall. I looked at Corey momentarily, and then we were pulled into the time portal.

"Zap!"

Chapter 42

May 3, 2022 – 11:55 AM

Karina, Garcia, and Wilma were in front of their computers, frantically searching for Corey and me as we traveled through the portal. They also monitored their screens dealing with energy surges within the portal and any changes within the time continuum.

"Beep!"

"Al just messaged me that they successfully stopped the intruders and sent them back to their respective historical time periods."

"Now that's great news, Kari."

"Do we need to find them at our end?"

"Yes, Garcia, we need their identities just in case they try to change the time continuum again or some other stunt that may cause a ripple through our time continuum or erratically change our true historical timeline."

"Ok, you got it, Kari."

"Garcia, let me know what you get while I check on Coach Hood's existence."

"Sounds good. Wilma and I will be busy with getting their contacts and identities."

In three minutes, they found that the intruders were two males at different time intervals. They were all unidentifiable because each of those intruders was an actual member of my team from a different historical time period. Their identities were constantly changing due to the flux within the time continuum. I won't be able to identify the intruders until the time continuum returns to its proper fixed position.

Soon after the discovery of those intruders, the glass chamber revved with a kaleidoscope of color lights static through the chamber from the sudden portal opening. Corey and I flowed through the door into the chamber. I checked my chronologies shown through the TVU to determine the historical time period we entered and whether the time continuum was restored. Exhausted and thrilled to return home, we exited the glass chamber, yet we were unsure we had corrected the time continuum to the last second. Yes, the large strokes of time were restored, but the finer points of time events within our lives and those interconnected with us were not returned to their original point. I discovered this unfortunate fact through our future missions.

After checking the settings of the Teleporter, I read the reports from Garcia, Wilma, and Karina and was satisfied that we saved the time continuum, at least with what we could observe. Even though Coach Hood's past was somewhat restored, I still had a naggy feeling that the time continuum was not one hundred percent corrected through that sudden mission. I just prayed that it was enough in our work to update our histories. The new mission I needed to complete was the salvation of Coach Hood. I had to wait at least seven days to prepare my head and heart for that new mission.

I Need You Today and Forever

by Redemption Group

Lord, have I missed the mark?
   Have I strayed away from You?
   Please do not take away Your Spirit from me
   Lord, I repent of my sins
   I need You today and forever.
   Oh, Holy God, I love You so
   I am lost without You in my life
   Like a boat without a rudder
   I cannot steer my life without You
   So, Lord, I pray to You for guidance and wisdom
   I don't want to be alone forever.
   Lord, have I been faithful to You?
   Have I proclaimed Your Word, Your Name,
   and shine for Your Son?
   Please don't say, "Begone, I never knew you."

I fear Your wrath, oh Lord.
So help me walk in Your way.
Oh, Lord Jesus, I need You today and forever.
Oh, Father God, I need You today and forever.
Oh, Holy Spirit, I need You today and forever.
Yahweh, help me with each second of my life.
I am lost without You, like a lamb without a shepherd
I need You today and forever.

Chapter 43

May 9, 2022– 1:45 PM

During this warm, sunny Spring afternoon, I walked to my favorite park – Washington Square Park. I looked at my cell phone screen, waiting for a response to my question. It's been ten minutes since I sent the text. Hey, waiting in this park was not so arduous compared to what I went through with my past missions. I sat down on a clean park bench and had an audible conversation with God. Thankfully, there was no one near me during our conversation. Of course, I whispered, just in case.

"Lord, I don't think he will show up. Do you think he will remember me at all?"

"He will show up. He needs closure in his heart of what he did to you and others, but he believes that no one will forgive him; he sees himself as unforgivable."

"Lord, I don't even believe he's forgivable, especially for all the abuse and sins he committed."

"Haven't you sinned, Albert?"

"Yes, of course, everyone sins. By the way, Lord, Coach Hood's sins were greater than mine, and I am good with You since I am saved."

"Albert, your sins are equal to Coach Hood's sins. Sin is an act against Me, and I do not give levels to sin in the final analysis. So, white lies are the same as real lies. Stealing money from your parent's secret hiding place is the same *as stealing from a bank or committing larceny from a company you work for. Sin is sin."*

"How about being saved? Would that give me a chance to go into Your Kingdom?"

"If you willfully sin with no remorse, tearful regret, or acknowledgment that you hurt Me, then you were never really saved. This means you will be tossed to Hell in that case. Everyone must walk in reverent fear of Me to fulfill their goals through Me. For those who cry out for forgiveness and try to repent of all sinful actions, they have a better chance to see my kingdom."

"Do I have any hope, Lord?"

"Yes, you do. Talking to Me and having a relationship with Me builds your faith in Me, bringing a deeper understanding of Me. In the end, this brings reverent fear. Furthermore, you need to read My Word, which is the instructions for all humanity and a great chance to know me."

"Buzz!"

I looked at my phone screen to find a reply to my question:

"Do you want to be free from your past sins, especially from all the pain you caused many children?"

Coach Hood replied, **"Yes!"** to that question. I sent a rendezvous time and spot in Washington Square Park. He replied,

"I will be there in ten minutes."

"Lord, give me Your Words to bring Coach Hood to You. Amen."

There was silence as I stood up from the bench I was sitting on when Coach Hood appeared, strolling with his head down without an attempt to look at my face. We didn't shake hands. Instead, we nodded and sat on the bench. In our conversation, I brought him back to the incident that changed me for most of my life. Because of his shame, Coach Hood shook his head and couldn't look at me. He asked that we could continue on another day. I said no as I gripped the books I was holding to.

I then talked about the Law Moses brought down from Mount Sinai and how God sent His Son to complete a business transaction. I told him,

"Jesus took our place on the cross and paid our fine, which was our sins. It stated in the first half of Romans 6:23, 'the wages of sin is death.'

Jesus died in our place for our sins, so we don't experience spiritual death."

I told him that he needed to repent and rely on Jesus for assistance in that repentance throughout his new life.

"Coach, the other half of Romans 6:23 was, 'but the free gift of God is eternal Life in Christ Jesus our Lord.' This is a promise which God cannot and will not break."

"Really? That is hard to believe."

"Yes, it's true. I have two Scriptures showing you God's seriousness in dealing with forgiveness from your sins. The first one is from Isaiah 43:25, 'I, I alone, am the one who wipes out your wrongdoings for My own sake, and I will not remember your sins.'

I talked about salvation for an hour, and Coach Hood accepted Jesus Christ with the assurance that He would come back and call us to His Home. Coach Hood was enthused with his decision and asked me to forgive him. I did, and we talked more about salvation for another hour, which included the following Scripture,

"As far as the east is from the west,

So far has He removed our wrongdoings from us."

He looked upon me with astonishment due to those Words. I tuned towards him and said,

"Coach, I need to get back to my wife. She is so pregnant that she is about to burst. We can get together again and review the Scriptures I have mentioned and others related to them."

"Oh, ok. What should I read?"

"You can read a chapter daily from the Gospel of John, Psalms, and Proverbs. This is a good way to start getting acquainted with God's Word."

"Ok, Albert, I'll start today on that. I do have an old Bible somewhere in my house."

I took out my Bible and turned to one of my favorite books.

"Good! Let me share a few Scriptures. The first one is from John 1:1 – 5. It states the following:

'In the beginning was the Word, and the Word was with God, and the Word was God. He was at the beginning with God. All things came into being through Him, and apart from Him, nothing came into being that has come into being. In Him was life, and the life was the Light of men. The Light shines in the darkness, and the darkness did not comprehend it.'

Jesus is the Word, Coach Hood. Don't hesitate to call me with any questions concerning this Bible passage or anything dealing with the Bible."

"Oh, I won't. Thanks again, Albert."

I extended my hand, and he hesitantly took it. We then walked from each other in opposite directions.

I Love You Jesus

by WWJD

My Lord Jesus
   My Lord Jesus
   I need You
   I love You, my Lord God
   Thank You my Lord God
   For saving me from eternal death
   Jesus, My Lord Jesus
   You are precious
   My Lord Jesus
   My King
   My Lord
   My God
   Jesus!
   I love You, Jesus!
   I love You, Jesus!

Chapter 44

I wrapped myself in a thick blanket and laid my head on my fluffy pillow. Then suddenly, my bed rocked back and forth. I raised my head to find myself on a boat. I looked down toward where my pillow should be, but to my surprise, I found a thick stack of sails.

"What's going on over here? How did I get on this boat? I must have traveled through the time portal to this place and historical period."

"Honey! Honey, get up!"

I raised my head after Karina nudged me for the third time,

"Huh? What's up, Kari?"

"Honey, my water broke. We need to go to the hospital."

"Huh? Are you sure?"

I rolled away from Karina and pulled the covers over my head.

"Our child is already seeking the center of attention. Why can't he wait until 9 AM or 10 AM to enter the world."

"Yes, and you better get a move on, mister."

Within 10 minutes, we drove down Queens Boulevard towards the Long Island Expressway. Once we got on the highway, driving Eastbound, the heavens opened, and I had trouble seeing through the sheets of rain during our frantic ride. There were enough cars on the highway, along with the intense precipitation, to impede our passage to the hospital.

"Al, please be careful. We need to get there in one piece," Karina called out from the rear seat.

"Don't you worry, sweetie. You're in safe hands."

I looked back through the rearview mirror for just a second. When I looked back towards the road, a car cut me off, which caused me to turn the steering wheel quickly and pump the brake hard; it was not the right thing to do in that situation. My car skidded.

"Hold on, Sweetie!"

"God help us!"

Karina yelled and held on to the window strap. I momentarily looked towards an overpass and saw a grey figure standing on it. It seemed to be observing our traffic predicament and upcoming doom.

"It can't be. I can't believe it. How did it find us? Why is it here? I thought we had taken care of that grey intruder?"

I shook my head in disbelief.

"Can't believe what, Al?"

"Nothing Kari. I am seeing things. Just hold on. We are going to hit a railing or a wall."

The figure was looking right at us with no concern for our situation. It was as if it was expecting us to skid through those three lanes. My car kept sliding over the wet road until we collided with a railing on the side of the highway. I looked back at Karina, and she was semi-conscious. I immediately called 911 and was told that an ambulance was approaching us. I entered the backseat to comfort my love and best friend until help arrived. After a few minutes of peace, serenity, and silence, a pair of bright lights grew more prominent and fast approached my car. I wrapped my arms around her shoulders and whispered,

"Kari, if you're awake, brace yourself against me. It looks like we're going to get hit."

"Boom!"

Index

The Scriptures were blended into the story to make it fluid in its presentation. In no way have I changed the accurate representation of God's Word.

Psalm 103: 12

John 1: 1 – 5

9 798987 703083